The Quilt Walk

The · Quilt Walk

By Sandra Dallas

PUBLISHED BY SLEEPING BEAR PRESS™

Library of Congress Cataloging-in-Publication Data

Dallas, Sandra.
The quilt walk / by Sandra Dallas.
p. cm.
Based on a story in The quilt that walked to Golden.
Summary: Ten-year-old Emmy Blue learns the true meaning
of friendship—and how to quilt—while making a harrowing wagon
journey from Illinois to Colorado with her family in the 1860s.
[1. Wagon trains—Fiction. 2. Frontier and pioneer life—Fiction. 3.
Quilting—Fiction. 4. Friendship—Fiction.] I. Dallas, Sandra.
Quilt that walked to Golden. II. Title.
PZ7.D1644Qu 2012
[Fic]—dc23
2012005863

ISBN 978-1-58536-800-6 (case)
10 9 8 7 6 5 4 3 2 1

This book was typeset in Sabon and Chanson d'Amour
Cover design by Mick Wiggins

Printed in the United States.

Sleeping Bear Press™

315 East Eisenhower Parkway, Suite 200
Ann Arbor, Michigan 48108

Sleeping Bear Press, a part of Cengage Learning.

visit us at www.sleepingbearpress.com

For Forrest, our "Golden" boy

HATCHETT ROUTE

Missouri R.

Iowa

Mississippi R.

Quincy

St. Joseph

Illinois

Kansas

Missouri R.

Missouri

Ohio R.

Golden

Quincy

CONTENTS

Chapter One

WE ARE GOING WEST

*W*e are going to Colorado!

Pa told us. He just came home from his first trip to Colorado Territory and announced that he and Ma and I were moving west to strike it rich.

Pa was gone almost a year. Gold had been discovered in the Rocky Mountains back in 1858, and four years after that, my pa, Thomas Hatchett, had gone off to find himself a mine. He'd promised to come home with a wheelbarrow full of nuggets. He didn't come back with any nuggets. He didn't even bring back a wheelbarrow. Instead he brought us the news that we were moving half across the country.

"We're moving where?" Ma asked.

"To Golden," Pa answered. "It's a town at the edge of the

Colorado Mountains, a booming place where we'll make a pot of money, Meggie." Ma's real name was Margaret, but everybody called her Meggie.

"Are there gold mines in Golden?"

"No, Meggie. The mines are in the mountains," Pa replied. "In Golden, the miners need places to buy their picks and shovels and gold pans, and to get their food supplies before they head off to the mountains. That means Golden will need stores, hotels, restaurants, offices, and banks. These businesses need someplace to set up. Golden is as bustling a place as you ever saw. I propose to build a business block. I'll make a fortune from 'mining the miners.' I'm going to load a wagon with construction supplies, and we'll go to Golden."

"By ourselves?" Ma sat down in her kitchen rocker, and I perched on the footstool.

"Not by ourselves. Will's coming, too." Will was Pa's brother.

"And Catherine? Did she agree to go?"

"Catherine is a dutiful wife," Pa said. "She will do as her husband says."

"I would never describe Catherine as dutiful. She is too independent," Ma said. She took a deep breath and leaned back in the rocker. Then she asked softly, "What you are saying is you expect *me* to be a dutiful wife. You made this decision without consulting me. What if I don't want to go, Thomas?"

Pa frowned at her. "You are my wife," he said. "You may stay if you wish, but I will not be here."

Pa's voice sounded harsh. Would he really leave us behind? I wondered. He had been away a year, and I'd been afraid that something had happened to him, that he'd gotten sick or had fallen off a mountain. Ma'd never said anything, but I knew she'd worried, too. What would we do if he abandoned us now?

"I have already made inquiries about selling the farm," Pa said. "Don't you see, Meggie. I can get enough for the place to buy the building materials and the wagons to transport them."

"I'll go, Pa, me and Skiddles," I said, hugging my cat. I talked in a small voice, because Pa didn't usually like me to speak up. Children should be seen and not heard, he told me often enough, although I was ten now and thought I had a right to voice my own opinions. I had learned a great deal about Colorado in school and knew it was a wild place, with gunslingers and Indians, outlaws and prospectors. Some of them had found gold just by throwing a hat on the ground and digging where it landed. It sounded much more exciting than Quincy, Illinois, the town closest to our farm. Here I was expected to act like a young lady, to sit and quilt with Ma and Aunt Catherine, and to practice my embroidery. Ma had sent me to a school for girls for a time, a place where I was supposed to learn to have fine manners and cross-stitch a sampler. There hadn't been enough money for me to continue. I didn't mind. I wasn't very good at sewing and had to take out so many of the cross-stitches that I thought my eyes would cross.

But those weren't the only reasons I spoke up. Ma would never let me go with Pa by myself. She'd have to come with us. We wouldn't be separated again.

Instead of reprimanding me, Pa smiled. He leaned over and took my mother's hands. "You see, Meggie, Emmy Blue knows we can get a start in Golden." His voice softened. "A new start is what we need, Meggie. What will happen if we lose the farm?"

"But the people I love are here," Ma said. "How can I leave my family, our neighbors? Will I ever sit and quilt with friends again? Moving west is a fine thing for a man. It means freedom and a chance for a better life for you. But it doesn't mean a thing to me. I'll be leaving behind everything I care about—home, church, school for Emmy Blue. Who knows if there are schools in Colorado, or churches?"

"If there aren't, you can start them. Come with me, Meggie. You will do well. You have a stout heart. It will be a better life, I promise."

"Do I have a choice? There is stubbornness in you as big as a mule." She looked sad, and I knew she was thinking not only about her family but about the graves in the cemetery, the ones we visited every Sunday. They were marked with a piece of white marble shaped like a tree stump.

Ma didn't talk much about her babies who had died. She said it wasn't proper. But I knew she grieved for them, and I did, too. I had loved them, especially my younger sister, whose tombstone read "Agnes Ruth, Our Sweet Baby Girl. Two Years, Three Months, and Seven Days." Pa would take Ma's hand as we stood beside the Hatchett graves. Then he'd sigh and put his other hand on my shoulder and say, "I'm glad we have you, Emmy Blue."

Once the decision was made to go to Colorado, Ma made up her mind to like it. She'd said about dandelions that if we couldn't do anything about them, we'd just have to enjoy them. That was the way she treated almost everything. If a thing couldn't be helped, she accepted it. Not that her parents did, though. Grandpa Bluestone told Pa he ought to be horse-whipped for taking Ma out where she could be killed by wild Indians, and Grandma Mouse cried and cried, and said she'd never see Ma or me again.

Grandma Mouse wasn't her real name. She was called that because she was so small—and because she had a pinched face and beady eyes like a mouse. She was really Emma Bluestone, and I was named for her. Only at the last minute, Ma told me, Pa rebelled at calling me exactly after Grandma Mouse, so he'd written my name in the Bible as *Emily* Bluestone Hatchett.

Perhaps it was a good thing I didn't have Grandma's full name, since I was not at all like her. She was tiny, while at ten years of age, I was already a good hand taller, with brown eyes unlike her blue ones. She was fine-boned, while I was gangly and awkward—unladylike, Grandma Mouse said. Ma called me high-spirited. "There is time enough for her to become a lady," she told Grandma Mouse.

"It wouldn't hurt for her to begin now. She could start by threading our needles for us. Nothing befits a lady more than fine stitching," Grandma Mouse said.

One day, then, when Ma's friends and neighbors, who made up her quilting circle, met at our house, Ma put my best friend, Abigail Stark, and me to work. We were told to sit under the quilt frame while the guests stitched, so that we could thread their needles. We sat there for an hour, the quilt above us, our hands sweaty as we tried to poke the thread through the eyes of the needles. As she licked the end of a thread, Abigail pointed to a woman's shoe, and I saw that it was untied. The shoe belonged to Miss Browning, a woman we disliked because she said we were disheveled urchins and told on us when we stole apples off her tree. I picked up her laces so gently that the woman did not feel it, at first meaning to tie them for her. But instead, I tied them to the laces of her other shoe. When the women stood up to roll the quilt, Miss Browning tripped and fell against a table, and her elbow landed in a plate of gingerbread Ma had set out. Then she knocked a display of pinecones, resting on the sideboard, to the floor, smashing them.

Grandma Mouse, who had glued the pinecones together, called us disgraceful and insisted we be punished. Miss Browning was unhurt, but she shrieked that the gingerbread had stained the elbow of her white blouse. So Ma, a look of fury on her face, took us both by our arms and dragged us down the hall and into the kitchen, shutting the door.

"Ma—" I began.

Ma put up her hand and shook her head. She clamped her hand over her mouth, because she had begun to laugh. Then she wiped her eyes, because she was laughing so hard, she had begun to cry. "You bad, bad girls," she said, and began to laugh again. "I have tried to find a way to get rid of those ugly pinecones ever since your grandmother gave them to us. Did you see the look on that pious Miss Browning's face? Did you notice how many of the other women smiled? Miss Browning is not a favorite among us, and she will never live this down."

Abigail looked at me as if there was something wrong with my mother. Ma caught the look and said, "You need not fear, Abigail. I have my wits about me." Then she took a broom handle and knocked it against a cushion on a chair. I understood her meaning, and cried out, "No, Ma. I'm sorry.

Don't whip me."

She pretended to make a few more whacks, then said, "This is our secret, girls. Now go to the barn to play where the ladies can't see you." Before she left, she cut a piece of gingerbread for each of us.

That was the last time that Grandma Mouse suggested I learn to sew.

"Emmy Blue is helping in other ways," Ma said whenever Grandma Mouse brought up the subject of my making a quilt to take to Golden.

"Well, I hope Colorado Territory is not so uncivilized that she will fail to become a proper young lady," was Grandma Mouse's reply.

That was exactly what I had hoped. And that was exactly why I was excited about going to Golden. After all, Golden was the Wild West. I'd be so busy watching out for Indians and hunting for gold that I'd never have to pick up a needle again.

Chapter Two

GETTING READY

Grandma Mouse and Grandpa Bluestone said Pa had no business taking Ma away from the farm, or me either, since it was the only home I'd ever known.

Ma would never say a word against Pa, especially to her mother, even if she didn't agree with him. "Colorado Territory is such a healthy place for Emmy Blue to grow up," Ma would say. "We'll leave all the damps of the Mississippi behind us. And my husband will have a chance to become a businessman. It might be a little difficult at first, but Thomas knows best."

"Best for whom?" Grandma Mouse sniffed. "Tom Hatchett thinks only—"

Ma cut her off. "I'll have you say naught about my

husband."

"But you're going as far away as the moon."

"Not so far, Mother."

"Well, it seems like it."

"How far is it, Ma?" I asked.

She thought a moment. "Farther than sunset."

Even though Grandma Mouse didn't approve of our moving to Colorado Territory, she was at our house almost every day, helping Ma make cheese and sauerkraut and pickles, and to smoke hams and cure bacon for our trip. The three of us gathered nuts and made dried apples. Ma bought molasses and vinegar, barrels of flour and sugar in big cones wrapped in blue paper. She'd soak the paper in water to make blue dye— in case Colorado didn't have dyes, she said. She packed bags of cornmeal and rice, coffee and tea, salt and saleratus, which some people called baking soda.

During the winter, Ma and Grandma Mouse and Aunt Catherine made candles and stitched sheets and pillowcases of dark cotton that wouldn't show the dirt. And the three of them pieced quilts.

Pa told Ma to leave the quilts behind. "They get tore up too easy," he said. But Ma put her foot down. "I'd as soon leave Emmy Blue behind as my quilts," she told him in such a strong voice that Pa put up his hands in surrender. Still, he complained that the wagons would be packed to overflowing.

Ma's quilts were special. She was known all over our part of Illinois for her fine stitching and precise piecework. She made a Feathered Star for her bed and a Twinkling Star for mine. Stars were her favorite design because, she said, we ought to sleep under stars. She'd even put a star into the baby-sized Medallion Quilt she'd made after my little sister Agnes Ruth died. Ma used scraps in it that were left over from the dresses she'd made for my sister. Before she quilted it, Ma had embroidered "Agnes Ruth, God's Precious Child, 1859" in the center. Sometimes she took out the memorial quilt and ran her hands over it, but she never put it on a bed. Nobody ever slept under Agnes Ruth's mourning quilt.

Pa worked as hard as Ma did to prepare for our move west. He and Uncle Will bought two sturdy Conestoga wagons, with big canvas covers stretched over hickory hoops and wheels that were made of narrow-grained oak. The wagons were big enough that Ma could stand up inside one. The men spread tar over the sides and bottoms of each of the wagons to keep out the water when we crossed rivers. They purchased lengths of pipe and kegs of nails; doorknobs and window latches; sheets of glass and fancy lumber for finishing the inside of the office block. And when spring came, they loaded it all into the two wagons, along with tools and a tent.

Meanwhile, Ma and Aunt Catherine set aside the food

supplies, the clothing, and our personal belongings. Grandma Mouse didn't want to help them pack, but I did.

"Why are you burying the teacups in the flour barrel, Ma?" I asked, watching her thrust one of her precious brown-white-and-gold Tea Leaf pattern cups deep into the flour.

"That'll keep them from getting broken. It's a long ride over hill and prairie and across rivers. If the wagon tips over, our cups will be safe," Ma replied, and laughed. "I hope we will be safe, too." She touched the end of her nose with her hand, leaving a trace of white flour. She looked like baking day.

Aunt Catherine handed Ma another cup and said to me, "Don't you remember we hid the silver teapot in the sack of rice so it wouldn't get banged up, and we buried the eggs in the cornmeal to keep them from cracking? And we stored the lucifers in a bottle with a cork so they wouldn't get wet?" She shook her head. "You can't start a fire with a wet match."

"We'll have to learn to adjust," Ma said. In fact, she had already begun to do just that. Pa told her she couldn't take both the tin plates and the china plates. One set would have to be left behind. Because she knew the china plates would get broken if we used them on the trail, she gave them to Grandma Mouse and packed the tin set.

"Adjust like you adjusted your skirts?" I asked. The two of them had hemmed their skirts well above their boot tops, which Grandma Mouse had said was scandalous. Ma did look odd in hers. She had gotten fat since Pa had come home, and the hems on the front of her dresses were uneven.

"Do you want me to be fashionable, or do you want me to let my skirts drag in the dirt and wear them out?" Ma asked me.

She smiled at me as she wiggled another teacup into the flour. "I have to say our skirts are now more comfortable, although I would not wish to enter Golden dressed in a skirt that topped my boots. When we get there, I will let down the hem on my best dress, the black one, for I want to make a good impression."

"On the Indians?" Aunt Catherine asked.

"Catherine," Ma warned. "I'm sure Colorado is perfectly civilized."

Pa came into the house then and looked at the foodstuffs in the kitchen. "Can't you cut down on some of it?" he asked.

"On what?" Ma replied. "Don't you want us to have enough food to reach Colorado Territory?"

"Then other things must go. We've packed and repacked. There isn't room."

"What do you want me to take out—the blankets and sheets, the skillet? I've already put aside the china plates, the rocker, and the washstand that was your wedding gift to me."

"Something else must go."

"There is only Emmy Blue. Do you propose to leave her behind?"

I looked up, my mouth open. They wouldn't leave me with Grandma Mouse, would they? When Ma saw the look on my face, she said she was only joking. "I wouldn't leave you. I love you as much as a wagon train of people," she whispered. Then she told Pa, "Perhaps you could leave off some of the fancy lumber."

"We need it. How will we build the business block without it?"

Pa glanced around the room at the boxes of foodstuffs that had not yet been loaded into the wagon. And then his eyes lit on the horsehair trunk, which had come from Grandma Mouse, her initials, EB, on the top, done in brass nails. She had given it to Ma for the journey, saying it would be mine one day, because EB were two of my initials, Emily Bluestone.

"The trunk," Pa said. "It will have to be left behind."

"It has our clothes in it."

Pa thought a moment. "Meggie …," he said.

Ma looked at him as if she knew what he was about to say. "No, Thomas," she said. "Not our clothes."

Pa looked away, then said, "You can take only the clothes you wear. There is no room for a trunk, no room for your clothes."

"But Thomas—"

"I have decided, Meggie."

Ma closed her eyes and took a deep breath, but she did not reply. She knew better than to argue with Pa when his mind was made up.

"Ma," I asked later. "Does that mean I can take only one dress?"

Ma did not answer. Instead, she opened the trunk and looked at the clothes neatly folded inside. "No, Emmy Blue, it does not." She slammed shut the trunk lid. "I have an idea, but we will not tell your pa. It will be a surprise."

Chapter Three

HO FOR COLORADO!

I didn't have the least idea what Ma meant until the next day when she woke me in the morning. I slipped on my new dress, the one she had made for me from blue calico, and buttoned it, but as I reached for my shoes, Ma said, "Not yet. Lift your arms."

I frowned at her, not knowing what she wanted, but I did as I was told and raised my arms.

Ma put my old red dress on top of the blue one and fastened it.

"What are you doing?" I asked.

"Your pa said we could take only the clothes on our backs. So we are wearing all of them. I promised your father we would wear them all the way to Golden. Now raise your

28

arms again. She picked up my third dress, the ugly brown one that I didn't like, and tugged it over my head. Then she covered me with two aprons.

"Do I have to wear both pairs of shoes?" I asked, and Ma laughed.

I looked closely at Ma then. She had on her yellow dress on top of her green one, and peeking out from under those two was her good black dress. All those clothes made her look fatter than ever. "Now button your shoes while I fix breakfast," she said.

A few minutes later I came down the stairs and said, "Waxy's ready to go." Waxy was a doll with a wax face that Grandma Mouse had given me. I was a little old for dolls, but I'd had Waxy ever since I could remember. She was a friend, and she might end up my only friend on the trip if there weren't any other children. Ma glanced at the doll, then began to laugh. "Oh my, Waxy is wearing all her clothes, too. And she has two hats on her head."

The neighbor women who had come to see us off gathered around and laughed at Waxy too, as fat as a cat in all her dresses and petticoats, although they seemed embarrassed that Ma was dressed that way. "How silly," one muttered.

"Why didn't you just hide your skirts in the flour barrel like you did the china cups?" another asked.

"Now, now," Ma said, for she would not abide any criticism of Pa. She smiled at the women and said, "Catherine and I agreed to this. I expect Catherine must be twice as big as I am, for she has twice as many clothes." We'd find out soon enough, because we would stop for Aunt Catherine and Uncle Will down the road.

The women drew their shawls about themselves in the cold morning. It was only March, but Pa said we had to get an early spring start. The earlier you go the more grass there is for your oxen. The men crowded around the wagon while Pa checked the contents a final time. He moved the last of the foodstuffs into the wagon, setting them beside the box that held the tin plates, forks, and ladle, a vinegar flask, the coffee grinder, and frying pan. The boxes were stored near the opening in the canvas wagon cover so that Ma could get to them each morning and evening. Pa's razor and shaving strop, Ma's candle molds, and other small items were stored in pockets Ma had sewn inside the wagon cover. Shovels and picks and coiled ropes hung from the inside of the wagon.

When he was satisfied, Pa drew the puckering strings attached to the wagon covers, and tied them tightly, leaving an oval-shaped opening, like a window at each end of the wagon.

I looked around for Abigail. She and her mother, who was Ma's closest friend, had promised to see us off. I saw them in the distance, hurrying toward us, each carrying something. At first I thought they were bringing Skiddles to say good-bye, but whatever they had wasn't wiggling.

The day before, when I had asked where we should place Skiddles' bowl in the wagon, Pa had looked at me strangely. "We can't take a cat with us, Emmy Blue."

I had stared at him. "Not take Skiddles? I've had him since I was a baby. Grandma Mouse gave him to me."

"I know you love that cat, but there's no way we can take him to Colorado. He'd get lost or eaten by a coyote. What if the wagon ran over him? He might even end up in an Indian's soup pot."

"Now, Thomas," Mother had warned. "No need to scare the girl."

"I'll carry him," I had said. "I'll hold him all the way to Golden."

"But you can't," Pa had told me, and as if to prove him right, Skiddles had jumped out of my arms and rushed through the door.

"I'm sorry, Emmy Blue," Pa had said gently. "You can't take a cat on such a long trip, and that's that. I thought your mother told you."

"I never," Ma'd said, but when she saw Pa frown, she had stopped. "We'll have to find him a good home, maybe with Abigail. She loves that cat."

"Skiddles is our family," I had cried, but Pa just shook his head, and I knew that Skiddles wasn't going into our wagon any more than the trunk with the EB initials on it. Ma and I took Skiddles and his bowl to the Stark house and asked if my friend would take him.

"Could we?" Abigail asked her mother.

"I guess one more cat wouldn't eat us out of house and home," Mrs. Stark said. "We'll take good care of him, Emmy."

When they reached us now, Abigail's mother thrust a bundle into Ma's arms. "I'm late because I had to add just one more stitch," she explained, and I realized she had brought us a quilt. Ma had tears in her eyes as she glanced at Pa, and I knew why. She was wondering how she could tell Mrs. Stark that there wasn't room in the wagon for anything more, especially a quilt. Pa had already fussed about the number of quilts we'd packed.

"Let's open it," Mrs. Stark said. Two of the women began to unfold the quilt. Others took the sides and spread it out. Ma looked at it and gasped. "Oh, my!" she said. "Oh, my, Emmy Blue, it's a Friendship Quilt." She looked around the circle of friends, her eyes shining. "You made this for me?"

"We wanted you to have it to remember us by. Each of us made a block and signed it. When you lie on the prairie at night, you can touch the names and think of us," said Mrs. Stark.

Ma turned to Pa and explained. "The pattern is called Chimney Sweep. We make these quilts so that friends going away won't forget us—as if I need a quilt to remember my dear friends!"

"We have stitched our heartache at your leaving into this quilt," Mrs. Stark said.

"I brought you something, too," Abigail whispered to me. She handed me a folded piece of cloth. I opened it and found a single Chimney Sweep square. "It's for Waxy. I made it myself," she said, although I already knew she had, because the corners didn't meet, and the stitching was uneven.

"Oh, Abigail, it's beautiful." I ran my hand over the square, just the way Ma had run her hand over the quilt, thinking what a wonderful gift this was. I knew Abigail didn't like to sew any more than I did. "But you didn't sign it."

"That's because I don't know how. I can't write, you know. But you can tell it's from me because of the bad stitching." Then she whispered, "I only just learned to thread a needle," and we both laughed, remembering our afternoon under the quilt frame.

As Ma was folding the quilt, Pa said, "There's not room to pack another thing, Meggie."

"Then I shall carry it," Ma said firmly. "Carry it or stay home. I may have to leave my friends behind, but I will not abandon their Friendship Quilt."

"Perhaps it will fit on top of the medicine chest then." Pa sighed as he took the precious quilt.

Just as we climbed onto the wagon seat, Grandpa Blue-stone and Grandma Mouse arrived. Pa grumbled that they were only making us late. Ma told him we were late because he had insisted on repacking the wagon.

Ma was happy to see her parents, and stepped on a spoke of the wagon wheel to get down off the box. Grandpa rushed to help her, giving Pa an angry look. "You could have waited. She'll need her mother and the other women when her time comes. And Emmy Blue, who knows what dangers she'll face."

"We've been over that, Father Bluestone," Pa said.

"Boy, you are taking your family into the jaws of death," Grandpa Bluestone told him. Grandpa was always saying things like that.

"Father," Ma said. "Thomas has taken every consideration for our safety."

"Humph," Grandpa protested. Then he took a deep breath and said, "I suppose you have indeed done that, Thomas. Well, if I can't talk you into staying, then I'll wish you luck."

"Emmy Blue, I almost forgot," Grandma Mouse interrupted. "I've got a surprise for you. You can open it after you cross the Missouri River and not a minute before."

"What is it?" I asked. Grandma Mouse gave me the best presents, well most of the time. She had given me white gloves and *The Girls' Own Book*, too. It told how little girls were to make themselves useful. (I was glad to leave that behind.) But she'd also given me Waxy and clothes for my doll, hair ribbons, and hard candy. Now she took a small calico seed bag from the basket in her wagon and handed it to me.

"Something for you to do as you travel west."

I began to loosen the drawstring on the bag, but Grandma Mouse said, "No, I told you not yet. You can't open it until you cross the Missouri River. With everything to see on the trail, you'll be too busy looking around to have time for it."

I started to put it into the pocket of my top dress, but Ma told me to secure it to the bottom dress instead, "So you won't be tempted to peek," she told me.

Grandma Mouse watched as I did so, then turned to Ma. "Meggie, I'll miss you." She wiped away tears.

"I'll write you letters, Mother," Ma said, rubbing her own eyes. "And I'll send them through the new overland mail delivery."

"It's not the same. You're our only daughter."

"You can take the train to visit us," I said, pleased that my suggestion would make them both feel better.

"There isn't any train. There isn't a train in the world that goes to Colorado Territory," Grandma Mouse said.

I'd never thought about that. I knew we were going a long way off. I knew we were traveling in a covered wagon, a "prairie schooner," Pa called it, because it was like a big ship and Pa had said we'd be driving it through a sea of grass. But until then, it hadn't occurred to me that we were going to a place so far away that no one could visit by train, only wagon.

I glanced around our farm, at the white house where I

had been born and lived all of my life, the place I called home. And suddenly our move to Golden didn't seem like such a wonderful adventure anymore. I looked up at my room, at the two windows with the pointed tops that made them look like church windows. For as long as I could remember, I had slept on the feather tick in that room, under a quilt with blue stars on it that Ma had made. Skiddles had slept on my feet, crawling under the covers on winter mornings to warm me. When I would wake at dawn, I would see Pa coming from the barn with a pail of milk or eggs that he had just gathered.

But now, Skiddles was gone, and we were leaving the house behind. In fact, it didn't belong to us any more. Pa had sold it to buy supplies for his business block in Golden. For the first time, I wondered where I would sleep after we reached Colorado. I reached for Ma's hand. I was confused about whether I wanted to go to Colorado Territory. Part of me was like Pa, wanting the excitement of going to a new place where we might become rich. But the other part wanted to stay in Quincy with my friends and grandparents, with everything I knew, where I would be safe. "Good-bye, little house," I whispered, my voice low and trembling.

- - - - - - - - -

It was mid-morning by the time we left Quincy. Pa shouted, "Ho for Colorado!" and tapped his whip on the rump of the lead ox, telling him to giddup. The six oxen started up, but they didn't go very fast. Pa said a two-legged dog could run faster than those oxen.

The crowd of neighbors stood aside to let us pass. "Be sure to send us some gold dust," a man told Pa.

"They say you need to take a wheelbarrow with you to haul all those solid-gold Pike's Peak nuggets," another yelled. Pa had told me the Colorado gold country was called "Pike's Peak" for a big mountain that the travelers could see from far away.

A neighbor asked Pa how many miles he expected to cover in a day, and Pa replied ten to fifteen.

"Well, now, won't that be traveling!" the neighbor said. "You'll go like the wind."

The women didn't call out. Instead, they stood silently, trying to smile, but they knew Ma would miss them. The women stood with Grandpa Bluestone and Grandma Mouse, who waved her handkerchief.

Abigail ran alongside the wagon until we reached the edge of our property. Then she stood at the fence post and waved. She took the arm of her doll and waved it, too, and I waved Waxy's arm back at her. Ma waved, also, but not Pa, who walked along beside the oxen, not looking back.

"We're off to Colorado," Pa said after the road turned,

blocking our view of the people who had come to see us off.

"We are indeed," Ma said, then turned to me. "We're off on an adventure, Emmy Blue. Do you know how many Americans would like to pull up stakes and go west? And we are lucky enough to do it."

Pa reached up and squeezed Ma's hand. "You'll see, Meggie. There's not a place in the world as beautiful as the mountains of Colorado. They'll be right at our doorstep."

Ma smiled, and I thought again about what she'd said about dandelions and learning to enjoy them if we couldn't do anything about them. I wondered if that strange place called Colorado Territory even had dandelions. I wondered if I should have brought some seeds.

Chapter Four

OUR JOURNEY BEGINS

e plodded along a road that was as familiar to me as the lane in front of our house, because we had visited my aunt and uncle on that road many times. The oxen were slow and didn't seem to like being yoked together, and I could have gotten there faster if I'd walked. At last we met up with Aunt Catherine and Uncle Will, and by then, I was hot under my three layers of clothes. Aunt Catherine looked hot, too, because they had been waiting at the end of their farm road since early morning.

"Thomas had to rearrange the wagon," Ma told Aunt Catherine, explaining our delay.

"Will was up in the middle of the night to repack ours, although I do not believe he found one more inch of space,"

Aunt Catherine said as she helped Ma down from the wagon. Wearing all her dresses, Aunt Catherine looked fat, although not as big as Ma.

Pa and Uncle Will walked around the oxen, checking the heavy wooden yokes, tightening the ropes on the wagon, which Pa had already tightened just before we left. Then the two of them leaned against Uncle Will's wagon and talked a moment about the road ahead. I was by myself on the wagon seat. Ma had Aunt Catherine, Pa had Uncle Will, but Skiddles was gone, and all I had was Waxy, who wasn't much for conversation. I wished again that Abigail and her parents could have gone west with us.

"You're all I've got, Waxy," I said. She just looked at me and didn't reply. Then because Waxy looked warm, I decided to take off one of her dresses. If she got too hot, her face would melt. I put the dress into the pocket of my top apron. Ma and Aunt Catherine and I might have to wear all our clothes, but I didn't see any reason why Waxy should. I was glad *I* wasn't in danger of melting.

"Westward ho!" Pa called at last, and I heard Aunt Catherine ask under her breath if Pa was going to talk like that all the way to Colorado. But I liked the sound of it, and I shouted back, "Westward ho, Pa."

He grinned and said, "How about walking alongside the oxen with me, Emmy Blue? It wouldn't hurt for you to learn to drive them."

"Isn't it dangerous?" Ma asked, climbing up the spokes of the wheel so that she could reach the wagon seat.

"More dangerous if she doesn't know. She needs to learn how to drive them, and you do, too, Meggie. After all, there will be times when I'll be called away—to hunt or to scout ahead. You and Emmy Blue will have charge of the wagon then."

"I suppose." Ma did not sound quite so sure.

Pa shouted, "Move out! Giddup!" to the oxen. He tapped the lead ox on the head with the handle of his whip. The two of us walked along beside the oxen as Pa explained the commands he gave them—"giddup" with a tap on the rump and "whoa" with a tap on the head. "Haw" with a touch on the right ear made the team turn left. "Gee" and a touch on the left ear made them turn right.

"Can you make them go backward?" I asked.

Pa nodded. "Tap the lead ox on the chest or the knees and yell, 'Back.'"

Pa warned me to stay out from under the animals' hooves. "Be careful around the wagon, too. With that heavy load, the wagon will kill you if you fall under it, or cripple you if it runs over your foot or your leg. There's more than one little girl that's got crushed by being run over by a wagon."

"Yes, Pa."

"And here's another thing. Don't jump off the wagon when it's moving. You could catch your dress and fall under the wheels."

"Dress*es*," I muttered, then said, "I won't get hurt."

We were keeping pace with the oxen, Pa walking next to them with his whip in his hand. He limped from a wound he'd gotten in the war, fighting for the Union. Pa'd enlisted in the war against the South as soon as it had started. He didn't believe anybody should be a slave, and that was why he'd joined up. But he'd gotten hurt in a battle and been discharged. The wound didn't seem to slow him much. He turned to look at me. "Emmy Blue, listen to what I say. There's plenty of danger on the trail, not just wagons and oxen, but runaway horses, rattlesnakes, fire, scorpions, floods—anything you can think of."

Pa looked at me hard, and that made me feel scared. "Are we going to make it?" I asked.

"Oh, we'll get there all right. I'm just telling you to be careful. Watch what you do, and don't run off. Wagon trains don't always wait for lost children."

"I've never been lost." It's true there were so many things to attract my attention that I often fell behind when I was out with Ma and Pa, but I'd never gotten lost.

"That's because you've never been anyplace that isn't familiar," Pa replied. "You've never seen a prairie. It's vast. It spreads from horizon to horizon with nary a tree or a house for a landmark. Why, sometimes, a person can't tell east from west. I know of grown men who've gotten confused in all that emptiness."

"Do they find their way home?"

"Oh, I guess most of them do, but often somebody has to go out looking for them."

"Is it scary, the prairie, that is?" I liked walking along with Pa. We'd never talked much before, because I'd been younger when he left for Colorado Territory the first time. After he came back, he was too busy planning for our trip west to pay much attention to me. He'd told Ma that the West would be a good place for me to grow up, but he'd never told *me* that.

Pa walked for a while in silence. "It can be scary when the storms come. It can thunder like the saints are firing Sharps rifles up in the sky, and there can be lightning like bolts out of hell. And then the rain will come, so thick you can't see from me to you. And when the storm is over, there's so much mud that you have to put blankets or quilts under the wagon wheels to get enough traction to move out of it. The mud's that thick, just like your ma's gravy."

I wondered what Ma would think if Pa put one of *her* quilts under a wagon wheel.

"It's beautiful, too," my father went on. "In the spring, the wildflowers on the prairie shine like a box of jewels. And the prairie grass in the fall turns the color of the gold the prospectors find in Colorado."

"Have you seen bad storms?"

"I have. I saw buffalo stampede, too. There were buffalo as far as you could see, as thick as prairie grass. Something starts them off, and the buffalo run and run all the way to tomorrow, sweeping up cattle and oxen."

"Well, they won't sweep up our oxen," I said. "Our oxen don't go fast enough to be swept up in a herd of turtles."

Pa laughed. He never laughed much. Lately, he worried about the farm, about getting ready for the trip, or about whether he could sell the farm for enough to buy the lumber and nails for the building in Golden.

He put his hand on my shoulder. "The trip west from the Missouri won't be easy, Emmy Blue, but there will be good things about it. The air's clean in Colorado Territory. There aren't any damps in the West like along the Mississippi River, no fogs or heavy mists that fill up your lungs, give you the malaria or the consumption. The sun comes out every morning, bright and yellow as a twenty-dollar gold piece. At least, I think so. I haven't seen a gold piece for a spell." He laughed again.

"And the people. I think I like that best of all about the West. There's gold to be discovered and stores to be built, money to be made, and they don't want to waste time. I think you'll like it, Emmy Blue. There's freedom out there, though maybe not yet for your ma. She likes quilting bees and tea parties, and Golden will have them one day if she'll give it time. You're more like me. I don't expect you'll mind too much if you can't sit in the parlor and thread needles, any more than I would."

I never thought I was like Pa, who could be moody and curt, and who made decisions without consulting Ma. As I walked along in the dust that the oxen stirred up, I realized I really was like him in some ways. I liked adventure. I didn't care for the idea of growing up to be like Grandma Mouse, sitting in her chair with her needle, never missing a thing that happened around her. I realized I was made up of both of my parents. I liked Ma's gentle ways, but like Pa, I was restless with all the rules about how girls had to behave. I was half of each of my parents, it seemed like the two of them were fighting inside me.

Chapter Five

SLEEPING ON THE GROUND

We didn't go very far that first day. We hadn't even reached the Mississippi when we stopped to camp. Aunt Catherine declared we should have spent one more night at home and left early in the morning so we'd have a full day of travel. "Why, I've a mind to walk back home and get the paring knife I left behind on the drain board this morning," she said. "I'd do it, too, if I didn't have to go all that way wearing every dress I own."

I wanted to tell her what was obvious, that she could take off the top dresses and Ma and I would keep an eye on them until she got back, but I wasn't sure Aunt Catherine would appreciate my speaking up. She had been in a complaining mood all day.

Ma didn't seem to mind that we'd gone only a little ways. She had practiced cooking over a campfire for a month, and she moved efficiently, taking the food box out of the back of the wagon and laying out the utensils. Of course, all she had to do was make coffee, since our neighbors had loaded us down with cakes and meat pies, boiled ham and fried chicken, bread, buttermilk, and boiled eggs. Pa had certainly found room for all that in the wagon. There was enough food for a week, Ma said, as she removed the food from the box.

Pa built a fire. Ma ground coffee and added it to the water in the pot, then set it on the coals to boil. Aunt Catherine sat down on a rock and held her hands over the fire. Since it was March, the weather, as in the mornings, was still cold at night. The smoke blew into her eyes, so Aunt Catherine moved to the other side of the fire. But the breeze changed directions, and the smoke drifted over there, too. "Smoke follows beauty," Ma said, but Aunt Catherine only grunted and waved the smoke away from her face.

When it was time for bed, Aunt Catherine said, "I never slept on the earth."

"Me neither. It's an adventure," I replied.

"More like a hardship," Aunt Catherine grumbled.

Pa sighed. I thought he ought to tell Ma that compared to Aunt Catherine, she was a good traveler, but Pa wasn't much for compliments. I curled up in my blanket and tried to go to sleep, but I wasn't used to sleeping on the ground, either, and it took awhile for me to settle in. So I lay there awake, listening to the sounds of the night—a dog howling, a cow mooing, birds cooing. It was dark, because the trees hid the stars, and the moon wasn't up yet.

After a bit, Pa whispered to Ma, "Aren't you going to sleep under that quilt those women gave you before we left this morning?"

"My Friendship Quilt?" Ma had been lying down, but now she sat up and faced Pa.

"I forgot that's what you called it."

"What else would you call a quilt made by your closest friends?" Ma asked. "Why, I'd rather go cold than put it down where it might get dirty."

"Well, it's a quilt, isn't it? What good is it if you can't use it?"

Ma sighed. "You don't understand, Thomas. A quilt's not just a bed cover. It's more than a collection of scraps. A quilt is a work of art. That quilt and my memories are all I have to remember my friends. Spreading the quilt in the dirt would be like my using one of your letters from the war to scribble a marketing list on."

"You saved them?" Pa asked.

Ma lay back down, and in the light of the moon, which had just come up, I could see her eyes were open. She turned toward me, and I shut my eyes, because I didn't want them to know I was listening. Ma said in a low voice, "Those letters are precious to me, Thomas. If something had happened to you, they would have been all I had left. Mother is keeping them for me until I can send for them. My Friendship Quilt is precious to me, too."

Pa didn't answer, and in a moment, I heard him snoring. I waited until I thought Ma was asleep, too, and then I got up and climbed into the wagon, removing the little quilt that Abigail had made for me. I wrapped it around Waxy, then held her in my arms and looked out at the sky until my eyelids were too heavy to stay open.

When I awoke, Ma was leaning over the campfire with the skillet. Aunt Catherine was taking her time folding her blankets and putting them into the wagon. Then she sat down on the wagon tongue and watched as Ma dished up breakfast for Pa and Uncle Will. "Come on, Cath. We still have yeast bread and fresh greens. Better eat up. It won't be long until all we have are beans and bacon, bacon and beans." Ma said.

Aunt Catherine just looked at Ma and didn't stand up. In a moment, Ma took her a plate of food and a tin cup of coffee. "We can't do a thing about our situation, so we'll have to enjoy it," Ma said.

Aunt Catherine didn't reply. Instead, she took a bite of food.

"Now where's Emmy Blue?" Ma asked. I sat up before Pa could poke me with his foot and tell me I was dawdling. "How did you sleep?" she asked me.

"The ground's lumpy," I said.

"No complaining," Pa ordered.

"I'm not complaining. Ma just asked me. I slept all right. It's Waxy who had a time of it. She wanted her feather mattress."

Uncle Will laughed at that. "You see, Cath, only fine ladies have trouble sleeping on the ground."

"I'm not a wax doll," she told him. "You didn't tell me when you asked me to go to Colorado that I'd have to sleep on the cold earth."

I frowned as I folded my blanket and put Waxy's quilt back inside the wagon. Where else did Aunt Catherine think we'd sleep? If the wagons didn't have room for our trunks, surely they wouldn't have room for beds.

Pa and Uncle Will yoked the oxen and we started off. The oxen were pokey, but I didn't care. I liked walking along beside the team with Pa. He knew the birds by their songs and told me the names of the ones that were singing. He identified insects that scurried across the road and pointed out animals that we saw in the bushes, plants, and among the toadstools.

We watched a turtle crawl along the road, going slower than the oxen. "Can I keep him for a pet?" I asked. After all, a turtle wouldn't run away.

"There's no room for pets," Pa told me.

I thought about Skiddles and hoped that he was happy. I

thought of Abigail and wondered if she missed me. I missed her.

At noontime, when the sun was highest in the sky, we stopped to let the oxen rest and we ate a cold midday meal. We still had plenty of food left from what the neighbors had given us, so dinner was a feast.

I was helping Ma store the leftover food in the box when I saw Uncle Will nudge Aunt Catherine with his elbow and point his chin toward Ma. "Do your part, Cath," he said. "You can't expect Meggie to do all the work in her condition. If you're going west with me, you'll have to pitch in."

I frowned, wondering what he meant by "her condition." Was he worried that Ma had gotten so fat she couldn't cook?

"I won't have Meggie waiting on you," Uncle Will continued. "There's time for you to go back. You could be home by nightfall if you walked fast. Make up your mind now."

I looked at Aunt Catherine, whose face was white as she stared at Uncle Will. "You'd go on without me?" she asked.

"That's the way of it. You've never been a shirker before, and I won't have it now."

Aunt Catherine didn't say a thing, only searched Uncle Will's face, until Ma called softly, "Cath, you're taller than I. Would you reach this box into the wagon. Honestly, I don't know why a wagon has to be this high. It wasn't designed by any woman, I can tell you that."

There was a long silence, and then Aunt Catherine said softly, "Yes, Meggie, I'll help you." She and Ma lifted the box into the wagon. While Pa and Uncle Will hitched up the oxen, Ma said, "Cath let's you and me walk for a time. My backside is sore from sitting on that board seat, and I bet yours is, too. Emmy Blue will take my place in our wagon, and I imagine Will can do without you. Those oxen don't need us. Besides, it's less than a mile to the river." When Aunt Catherine hesitated, Ma said, "What would I do without you, Catherine? The only reason I didn't put up a bigger fuss about going west was I knew you'd be with me."

The two of them started out ahead of us. Then Uncle Will lifted me into our wagon. As he did so, he said to Pa, "Your wife's quite a woman. I think Catherine might have walked all the way back home if it weren't for Meggie."

"Oh, she'd have gone with you," Pa said.

Later, as Pa walked beside me, flicking his whip at the oxen, I asked, "Do you really think Aunt Catherine will stay with us instead of going back home?" I hoped she wouldn't leave, because Ma would indeed be lonely without another woman.

"Of course, she'll stay with us. A woman's to go wherever her husband goes. You remember that, Emmy Blue."

"But what if she'd gone back and taken Ma with her?"

Pa laughed and told me, "Your ma knows her duty."

He went up to the lead ox then, and when he could no longer hear me, I said to my doll, "Let's think a long time before we get married, Waxy."

Chapter Six

ACROSS THE MISSISSIPPI

We reached the Mississippi in the early afternoon, and it took us the rest of the day to cross it. The Mississippi river was a mile wide, far too wide for the animals to swim across. Besides, Pa said, we'd only just started out.

So we took the ferry across. It was a large, flat boat, like a giant raft, and it was big enough for more than one wagon, but many people were ahead of us, so we had to wait our turn. I'd seen the Mississippi plenty of times, but I was still awed by how wide it was. I remembered Pa talking about the size of the buffalo herds and wondered if a herd could fill up the river. If so, we could drive across on their backs, instead of waiting for the ferry.

We took our place in the line of prairie schooners at the

ferry landing. We pulled in behind a wagon with a dairy cow tied to the back. Ma and I climbed down, and Ma patted the cow on the side. "Soo, Bossy," she said. "We sold our cows before we left. I miss fresh milk already," Ma told the woman from the wagon.

"I'd share with you, but the young 'uns drank up what we got from the morning milking, and I used the cream to make butter," the woman said.

"Where in the world do you find time to churn?" Ma asked.

"Oh, I don't." The woman went to a bucket hanging from the back of the wagon and lifted the lid. "Lookit here. I put the cream in this morning, and the rocking of the wagon churned it for me."

Ma and I peered into the bucket and saw clumps of yellow butter. "Why, I expect that's the best thing yet I've heard about going to Colorado Territory!" Ma said.

The woman beamed and sat down on our wagon tongue, pulling a quilt square from her pocket. "This is what I like best. There's time to do my piecing while I'm sitting on the wagon seat. I guess I'll have the whole quilt done by the time we reach the gold country."

"What a fine idea," Ma cried. "Emmy Blue, look at her cunning stitches."

"You stitch, do you?" the woman asked.

"Ma likes it better than supper," I piped up.

The woman laughed. "That's the way of it, isn't it? I guess I can make my home anywhere if I have my quilting."

"Let me show you something," Ma said, and she went to the back of our wagon and took down the Friendship Quilt. I helped her unfold it and hold it out, and the woman ran her hand over the squares, touching the embroidered names. "Why, there's nothing in the world I'd treasure more. It's like taking home with you all the way to the gold fields," she said.

"What a lovely way to put it!" Ma replied. The two of them chatted until we reached the water's edge.

When our turn came for the ferry, Pa and Uncle Will drove the wagons onto the big wooden platform made of boards and propelled by men with long poles. The ferrymen pushed off, and in a moment, we were on the muddy water, making our way to the other side of the Mississippi. I stared upstream, watching for trees in the current that would overturn the raft, then turned and looked at the Illinois shore as it got smaller and smaller.

"What do you think of this for an adventure?" Pa asked.

I wanted to tell him it was scary, that I was afraid one of the oxen would bump up against me and push me into the river. The water was so dirty, no one would ever see me if I went under. But I didn't want to admit I was afraid, so I asked, "Does Colorado have big rivers like this?"

"Only the Platte, but it isn't much of a river, a mile wide but only an inch deep, they say," Pa told me.

"Then I wouldn't mind falling into it," I told him.

"Hold on to the wagon wheel. It's chained to the ferry. Don't you worry, Emmy Blue. These river rats know what they're doing," he told me, and pointed with his chin to the two men in charge of the raft.

I turned and watched the Missouri side of the river come closer and closer, until finally we bumped against the shore. Pa and Uncle Will led the oxen off the ferry, and before I knew it, we were looking for a campsite.

"Ho for Colorado!" Pa said. I didn't respond this time. Like Aunt Catherine, I was beginning to get tired of hearing that.

Pa said we were making good time through Missouri, going twelve or fifteen miles a day. Horses would have gone faster, but oxen were better suited for the Great Plains, even if they were slow and too stupid to swat flies with their tails. Another advantage, Pa said, was that while the Indians might shoot oxen, they wouldn't steal them because they had no use for them. Even Aunt Catherine laughed at the idea of an Indian man on an ox, riding across the prairie.

"Wouldn't they eat them?" I asked.

"They'd have to be awfully hungry," Pa replied.

Aunt Catherine perked up after we crossed the Mississippi.

Every day she was happier and more helpful, and she even made jokes, asking, "If we just crossed Mrs. Sippi, where do you suppose Mr. Sippi has got to?"

Uncle Will slapped his knee and laughed. The joke wasn't all that funny. I think he was just glad that Aunt Catherine was back to her old self.

Aunt Catherine began doing some of the cooking, telling Ma, "Now, Meggie, you know you shouldn't overdo it. Save your strength. You'll need it."

"What's wrong with you, Ma?" I asked.

"Oh, I'm fine, Emmy Blue. Don't you worry about me."

Pa said to enjoy the trip while we could, because it would get harder once we were through Missouri and across the Missouri River. "These are easy days," he said, and they were. The road was smooth, with farms along the way. Sometimes we stopped at barnyard wells to water the stock, and the farm wives invited us to rest a spell.

The farmers gathered around the wagons and asked Pa and Uncle Will where they were going. "You been to Colorado before? You find a mine, did you?" one asked.

"Why, I'd give you this whole farm for just one bucket of Pike's Peak nuggets," another farmer said.

At a farm where several children played, a girl about my age asked me, "You like going west?"

"It's better than threading needles for Ma's quilting group," I told her.

The girl giggled. "I don't care for that, either. What's it like riding in a covered wagon?"

"I walk with Pa most of the time," I said, feeling grown up. "Who wants to sit on a seat as hard as a milking stool all day?"

"I guess you like it right well."

"I guess I do."

Ma and Aunt Catherine talked with the women. "Why'd you agree to uproot and go to Colorado?" one asked them.

Ma replied, "We thought we'd have a better living out there."

But another woman said, "Laws, how I'd like to go along. Sometimes I think if I have to gather one more egg, I'll throw it to the cats and take off walking. Imagine the chance to look in a gold pan and find a thousand dollars."

"You'd give up your home?" Aunt Catherine asked.

"Faster than you could say, 'Pickled peppers.'"

After we were on our way again, Aunt Catherine asked Ma, "Do you think that woman would run off?"

Ma laughed, but then she turned and looked back in the direction of the farm. "Maybe not this afternoon, but I wouldn't be surprised if we spotted her in Golden one day."

Chapter Seven

OUR ADVENTURE IN ST. JOE

The weather was good in Missouri, warm but not hot enough to make us uncomfortable in all our clothes. Even though there was a tiny bit of room in the wagon, now that we had eaten some of the food given to us by our neighbors and friends. Ma still insisted we wear all our clothes. I heard her tell Aunt Catherine she was afraid Pa would make her throw out the extra dresses if she asked to store them in the Conestoga. "We'll wait. I promised I'd wear all the dresses," she said.

"I think Thomas would find room now if you asked him."

"Well, I won't," Ma said. "I believe he and Will must have laughed at us wearing all these clothes, thinking we'd beg for a place to store them. Well, we'll show them."

"*We?*" Aunt Catherine asked, and laughed. "Thomas is not the only one who is stubborn."

So far we didn't have worries from Indians, we were able to find water, and we didn't run into any rattlesnakes, as Pa thought we would, and it seemed like we flew as fast as birds across the state. It wasn't even a month—it was April now—before we reached St. Joseph, or St. Joe. That's where Pa said we would get the plans for the business block. He had written to a friend who was set up in St. Joe as a builder and had promised to draw them up. We would hook up with a wagon train there, too.

"We've done all right on our own. Why do we need to join a train with all that dust and animals milling around and not a moment of privacy?" Aunt Catherine asked.

"It's dangerous to cross alone. There are Indians, and what if one of us fell under the wagon or got snake bit? Neither Will nor I know about doctoring. And if the wagon breaks down, there'll be someone to help us. Besides, Meggie ought to have other women with her," Pa explained.

We had found a place along the east side of the Missouri River to camp. It was filled with wagons and tents, and Pa went in search of a wagon train to join. He came back an hour later and told us, "Good news! There is a train leaving in two days for Denver City, which is the big town close to Golden. We are welcome to join it. All we have to do is get ourselves across the river." I was too big to be picked up, but

Pa did just that. "Emmy Blue, there are children in that train, so you won't have to spend your time with us old people."

We had passed through the streets of St. Joe on our way to the camp, and I was anxious to explore the town. I'd seen men in buckskin pants embroidered with beads and a family of Indians sitting in the dirt, begging for "beeskit."

"Look, Indians," I'd cried.

Pa shook his head. "The coming of the white man has not been a good thing for those poor folks. You'll see grand Indians out on the plains, Emmy Blue, the finest specimen of men, whose skill with horses beats any I ever saw. But these Indians"—he nodded at the family—"are no more than dirty beggars, as bad as any white bum you ever saw at home. The men—and the women, too—are addicted to whiskey."

"You mean they're like Betsy Pride's father?" Betsy was a girl who lived in a shack with her father on a rundown farm not far from where we had lived. Her mother was dead, her brother had run off, and she lived alone with her father, who was a drunkard. Sometimes Ma hired Betsy to help with the cleaning and the cooking. Ma treated her kindly. She gave her a dress she said she was tired of, combed her hair to get out the twigs and burs, and insisted she spend the night when she worked late. I thought she was the sorriest girl I ever met and asked Ma what I could do.

"Be a friend to her," Ma had said.

And so whenever I met her on the street, I was friendly.

Once when Abigail and I took a picnic into the woods, I invited Betsy to go with us, although she was almost a grown-up. She taught me how to shoot marbles and whittle with a knife.

"Yes, these Indians are no better than Betsy Pride's father," Pa told me. "He was a worthless old thing."

"Who?" Ma asked, coming up to us.

"We were talking about Hal Pride."

Ma shook her head. "Poor Betsy. She never had a chance."

"Will and I are going into town," Pa said, changing the subject. "St. Joe is no place for a lady. Besides, somebody has to stay and guard the wagons. Who knows what could be stolen."

I was disappointed, because I wanted to see St. Joe. I didn't care that it was rough or that bad people lived there. But I knew better than to beg Pa to go.

"I'll stay," Ma said, and I knew that was the end of it.

As Ma and I watched the men go off, Aunt Catherine came up to us. "They're going without us?" she asked.

"I promised to watch the wagons. Besides, Thomas says St. Joe is no place for a lady."

Aunt Catherine put her hands on her hips. "I didn't promise any such thing. And if your husband believes it is all right for a lady to face drought and wind and Indians and wild animals, I see no reason why we should be protected against whatever dangers St. Joe has. After these dull days, I would welcome a bit of excitement. Come along, Emmy Blue.

I am in need of a spool of thread, which I daresay your Uncle Will would approve of because he has torn his shirt and I have nothing to stitch it up with. You and I can see the sights on the way to the store."

I stared at her, my mouth open. Then I turned to Ma, who would surely say no. But instead, Ma smiled at me. "I promised *I* would stay. I didn't say anything about you. It may be your last look at civilization, such as it is. But try to come back ahead of the men."

So Aunt Catherine took my hand, and we walked toward the center of St. Joe, making sure we kept well behind Pa and Uncle Will.

St. Joe wasn't that much different from Quincy, the town near our farm that we'd visit two or three times a year. In fact, it wasn't even as nice. There were new brick buildings and a big hotel on streets that were dusty and rutted from the wagons passing through. Houses were being built of brick and stone. The town was crowded with people dressed in all sorts of clothing—overalls, suits, fur, and buckskin embroidered with beads and pieces of calico. There were ladies in lace and satin and men in flowered vests under what Aunt Catherine called frock coats. As I stopped to take everything in, a delivery wagon shot past us, churning mud. I jumped back as the driver yelled, "Watch it, girlie."

We passed outfitting stores with tents, frying pans, rope, and wagon wheels. There were big shallow pans that Aunt

Catherine said the prospectors used to wash gold out of the streams and there were picks for breaking rock. I saw heavy work pants and felt hats, rows of canned tomatoes and oysters and sardines. Sombreros and paper collars were piled on counters next to stacks of ammunition. And everywhere—on the counters, in windows, piled on top of bins of spices—were guidebooks to the Pike's Peak country.

After visiting several places, we found a dry goods store and went inside, where Aunt Catherine fussed over the ribbons, selecting one that was a lavender plaid. "I'll keep this in my pocket and take it out when no one is looking so that I'll know I'm still a lady," she said. "Now, Emmy Blue, pick out a ribbon for your braids."

"Truly?" I asked. I had not brought hair ribbons with me.

"Of course. I have a little money of my own, and I expect to spend it frivolously. Who knows when I'll ever have a chance to be carefree again? Choose a ribbon for Waxy, too."

I went through the ribbons carefully, narrowing my choice to a yellow that was the color of the morning sun and a blue the color of the late afternoon sky. "Blue. It won't show the dirt," Aunt Catherine said when I asked her opinion. "But I believe Waxy would like the yellow."

A clerk cut the ribbons for us, and Aunt Catherine added a packet of pins and a piece of red calico for Ma.

"What about the thread?" I asked as we left the store.

"Thread?" She looked confused. "I have plenty of thread.

We don't need any more thread."

"But you said you needed some."

"Oh, I did, didn't I?" She smiled at me. "I guess your ma won't mind that little fib. Bother about thread! Now, let's go sit down in real chairs and have real tea," she said, looking approvingly at the Patee House, a fine brick hotel across the street. "Surely they have a ladies ordinary."

"A what?" I asked.

"It's a tea room reserved for women, a place where we can sit and relax. There is one at the Quincy House at home." She took my hand and led me across the street, through the lobby of the hotel into a room that was fitted with fragile chairs and tables. I felt out of place, because I still wore three dresses, but Aunt Catherine moved like a queen past the ladies in their fashionable frocks and bonnets. When I glanced around, I saw other women dressed in traveling clothes.

Aunt Catherine ordered tea and tiny cakes, and I perched on my chair trying to act ladylike and not put the entire cake into my mouth at one time.

"Going west are you?" asked a lady at the table next to us.

"We are," Aunt Catherine replied. "And you?"

The woman nodded. "This is my wedding trip. I don't suppose I'll find tea and pastries in Denver."

"We are going to Golden. We leave in two days," Aunt Catherine told her.

"Why, maybe we'll be on the same train." The woman

wiped her fingers on her napkin. Her hands were already brown and rough. "I am Lucy Bonner."

Aunt Catherine told her our names, and the two of them chatted, but not for long. We had to return to the wagon before Pa and Uncle Will got back. So we took our leave. Aunt Catherine ordered three little cakes to take with us and put them into her bag.

Ma smiled when she saw the cakes, and the three of us sat on the wagon tongue, and we took tiny bites to make them last longer. We ate every crumb.

"Do you think we should have gotten cakes for Pa and Uncle Will?" I asked.

"No," Ma and Aunt Catherine said together. Then the three of us began to laugh. I knew without their telling me that I should not mention our outing. That night, I told Waxy that I was learning something about how women keep secrets.

Chapter Eight

CROSSING THE MISSOURI

*T*he Missouri wasn't as wide as the Mississippi, but we still took a ferry to cross it. Pa said some people might let their oxen swim across, pulling the wagons, but he didn't want to take a chance we'd overturn.

"Isn't a ferry just as liable to tip over as a wagon?" Aunt Catherine asked.

"The ferries are stable," Uncle Will told her. "Don't you remember we took the ferry across the Mississippi?"

"I had my eyes closed the whole time," she said.

"We'll float across some of the smaller rivers later on," Pa said. "That's why we spread tar on the bottoms of the wagons before we left. They are tight as washbasins. We'll be as dry as if we were on a steamboat."

Early in the morning, we gathered with the other members of our wagon train. Ma nodded at some of the women, and Pa greeted one or two men he'd already met, but there wasn't time to talk. We had to get across the Missouri, and Pa said that with all the wagons, the crossing could take the entire day. Our wagon master had already hired a guide, a man who was called Buttermilk John. He'd crossed the plains a dozen times before, and he would be our scout. He said he'd wake us up at dawn so we could get an early start. We'd stop at noon—*nooning*, he called it—then camp for the night when he found the right spot. Pa and the others would take turns being guards.

Buttermilk John looked like an Indian. He was dressed in a buckskin suit and moccasins, and his long hair was tied back with a strip of indigo calico. Pa said Buttermilk John's looks didn't matter. He was a good man who would get us through safely to Colorado Territory.

"Ye've got quite a load, old son," Buttermilk John told Pa, when he inspected our wagon at the river. "I hope you don't sink the ferry."

"Thomas knows best," Mother said.

"He was just joking," Pa told her.

Ma asked, "Where should Emmy Blue ride, beside the wagon or on the seat with us?"

"On the seat, high up, where she can see."

The Missouri was filled with ferries taking across prairie

schooners and men on horseback. There were also dugouts, canoes manned by Indians. We'd seen the Indians racing their horses back and forth along the river when we were camped. Now they seemed to want to cross with us, and they pushed their boats alongside the ferries.

These Indians weren't like the family of beggars we'd seen in St. Joseph. They were shirtless or else wore faded calico tops and had feathers and bits of bright cloth woven into their hair. They hailed us, begging for "beeskit, tobac, ko-fee." They offered to row some of our load to the far side, but Pa said he wasn't about to transfer anything in the middle of the Missouri River.

Ma held so tightly to the wagon seat that her knuckles lost their color, and I remembered that she couldn't swim. I worried that if the wagon tipped over, she'd be lost in the brown river, maybe kicked by the oxen, who were churning the muddy water. Then I remembered I couldn't swim either, and I grabbed hold of the seat as I looked into the water that was swirling and foaming from all the traffic. The river was as busy as downtown Quincy on Saturdays.

The river current was strong, and our ferry drifted downstream. Pa said he wasn't worried. He told us it mattered more that we got across the river than where we ended up. The ferry landed, and Pa jumped out of the wagon and gathered the oxen, which had swum across beside us. Then he went back to the river to look for Uncle Will, but he couldn't see him. "We'll go on to the gathering place. He'll likely be there," Pa said.

Pa helped Ma and me down from the wagon, and we shook our skirts because they had gotten wet. We started to walk, but even though we had hemmed our dresses above our boot tops, the fabric was wet and dragged in the dirt.

"We'd best ride until we dry out, or our clothes will be covered with mud," Ma said. So we climbed back onto the wagon and spread out our skirts to let the sun warm them.

We headed up the river to where the rest of the wagon train was gathering and finally found Uncle Will and Aunt Catherine. "Thank the Lord you're all right, Meggie," Aunt Catherine said. "I got to thinking, what if you were lost? I couldn't bear it." She lowered her voice. "I thank God you are with me, you and Emmy Blue. However could I go to Colorado Territory without you?"

"Or we you," Ma replied.

Buttermilk John had crossed the river and told everyone to keep on going. "We won't camp on the river for fear of 'quitoes. They're big as horseflies," he said. So we followed the other wagons a mile or two farther on, to a meadow. Those who'd crossed before us had already unpacked their wagons and spread their things on the ground to dry, because even the best wagons had taken on a little water.

"Ye made it did ye, Hatchett?" Buttermilk John said as he rode up to our wagon.

"Said I would," Pa replied. But he added, "We took some water. I hadn't expected that."

"This is the hardest crossing 'tween here and Denver City," Buttermilk John said. "We'll have to cross the Platte River a time or three or four, but it's not so deep, nothing a wagon like yours can't handle. Look at that wagon over there." Buttermilk John pointed with his chin. "The wagon's made of green wood. This child thinks they'll be lucky to make it halfway across the plains, if they don't break down before."

Buttermilk John went on to the next wagon, and I asked Pa, "How come he calls himself 'this child' and you 'old son?'"

"He's a mountain man. They talk that way."

"What's a mountain man?" I'd never heard of one.

"An old-time trapper. The trappers were the first white men in the West. They caught beaver and other animals for their fur. But the West has been trapped out. The animals were plentiful in the 1820s and '30s, when the mountain men first arrived, but not now. Besides, with all the settlers coming in, there isn't room for the mountain men anymore. So they work as guides. Some of them married Indian women and lived with the tribes. Their wives make their buckskin suits and bead them, making holes in the buckskin with a tool called an awl. Those Indian women work harder than any woman I ever met, except maybe your ma."

I decided to tell Ma what Pa had said because he didn't praise her very often.

After our wagon was unpacked and our wet things spread on the ground to dry, Pa and Uncle Will went to a meeting with the other men in the wagon train. A woman came over to Ma and Aunt Catherine and introduced herself. "I'm Esther Reid from Illinois, and we're headed to Georgetown, Colorado, where we expect to find a gold mine. My husband does, at any rate. Me, I'd be happy to find a cabin with a feather bed to sleep on—that is, if there are feathers in Colorado."

Aunt Catherine sat down on a box and took off her sunbonnet. "A feather bed would be nice, but I think I would like best to have a cook stove." She'd burned the hem of one of her dresses in our campfire the first week out.

"A rocking chair. That's what I'd like," Ma said.

"You can come sit in mine any time you care to," Mrs. Reid said to Ma. "I told my husband I'd as soon leave behind a wagon wheel as that chair. I have him take it down every night. That way I can sit by the fire with the Good Book and my piecing. I'm just as happy as if I was back at home."

"It seems all of us have brought our piecing," Ma said. "I do mine sitting on the wagon seat, and I've observed women stitch as they walk along."

"Quilting's a woman's way of dealing with troubles. There's nothing so bad that piecing with the colors doesn't help," Mrs. Reid said. "Working with a needle in my hand brings me peace."

"Amen," Aunt Catherine said.

"Does the young 'un quilt?" Mrs. Reid asked, looking over at me.

Ma looked to me to answer for myself, and I squirmed. "Not really," I said.

"I believe she'd rather hunt insects and toadstools than sit with her quilting," Ma explained.

"Of course, what troubles does a girl that age have? Nothing at all for her to worry about."

"I think she might miss her home just a little," Ma said.

I was pleased Ma remembered how much I'd missed our farm when we'd started out, although I didn't think about it as much now.

Just then, another lady walked up and said, "Mrs. Hatchett." Both Ma and Aunt Catherine were Mrs. Hatchett, because Pa and Uncle Will were brothers, so both of them turned to her.

"Mrs. Bonner," Aunt Catherine said, recognizing the woman we'd met at the Patee House. She explained to Ma, "Mrs. Bonner sneaked off for tea, too. But she is a newly married woman, so I suppose her husband indulges her."

Mrs. Bonner looked at the ground. "Owen was very angry and called me a common woman for going off by myself like that. He said I must ask his permission. He was right to punish me."

"Punish you?" Aunt Catherine frowned.

"He said I am to sit in the wagon all day today and tomorrow and not be allowed to walk. He knows how I love to walk along. I am here only because he sent me to ask for the loan of a hammer."

"Why of course," Ma said. As Ma climbed into the wagon, Mrs. Bonner turned, and I could see bruises on her cheek. "You've hurt yourself," Ma said, then put her hand over her mouth as if she should not have spoken.

"I am clumsy. I fell," Mrs. Bonner said in a low voice, putting her hand to her cheek. "I must get back. Owen does not like me to be gone. I'll return the hammer when he has finished." She turned toward her wagon, and then said, "I can see he's not there. He must have left with the other men to attend a meeting with Buttermilk John. I am glad to be with other women."

"How long have you been married?" Ma asked.

"We wed only before we left for Colorado Territory, in Fort Madison, Iowa."

"Where's your husband from?" Aunt Catherine asked.

Mrs. Bonner frowned. "I am not just sure. Owen has lived many places, he says. He does not like me to question him. We met in person only the day before the wedding."

"You are a mail-order bride?" Aunt Catherine asked.

I'd heard about such women. Men advertised in the newspapers for ladies who wanted to get married and go west. If

a woman was interested, she wrote to the address in the ad.
I'd even read one of those ads in Pa's paper to Abigail, and
we had wondered who would answer it.

"Oh no. I did not answer an advertisement in the news-
paper for a wife. I would never do that. Owen wrote to our
minister, asking for the name of a woman who would cor-
respond with him with the thought of matrimony, which I
believe is entirely proper. And the minister gave the letter
to me because, I suppose, I am twenty and eight and was well
on my way to becoming a spinster." She turned to me and
added with a little laugh, "That means an old maid." Then
she continued, "Owen wrote such beautiful letters. He said
he had business in Colorado Territory near Golden—."

"Golden?" Ma interrupted.

"Do you know it?"

"Why, we are going to Golden ourselves, Catherine and
I. Our husbands are going to build a business block there."

"Then we shall be friends," Mrs. Bonner said. "Oh, I am
happy." She stopped a moment and looked at the ground.
"That is, if Owen approves. He says he likes to have me to
himself."

"That's the way of most new husbands," Aunt Catherine
said. "You can get to know him better that way."

"Yes, I must learn to please him," Mrs. Bonner said. "He
seemed like such a gentle man in his letters."

"You will tell us if you need anything," Ma said.

As Ma, Aunt Catherine, and I watched her go, Aunt Catherine said, "I hope we can be her friends. She seems a well-bred person."

"What happened to her face?" I asked.

"When you're older—" Ma began, but Aunt Catherine interrupted her.

"Emmy Blue's out in the world now. She should know about such things."

"I suppose you're right," Ma said with a tinge of sadness in her voice.

"Some men are brutes," Aunt Catherine said, and then added quickly, "but most men are good, like your pa and your uncle. They'd no more lay a hand on us than they would fly over the barn. But there are men, Emmy Blue, who hit their wives."

I'd never heard of such a thing and was shocked. I couldn't wait to tell Waxy about that! She'd be as disgusted as I was. When Aunt Catherine had threatened to go back home, Uncle Will had only raised his voice and certainly not his hand. Then I remembered my friend in Quincy. "You mean like when Mr. Pride hit Betsy?" When I'd learned about that, I'd been sick at heart. My pa had never so much as switched me with the cane he used when he was first wounded. He would never do such a thing.

Ma nodded. "They are evil men. I don't know what makes them that way."

"Did she do something that made him angry?" I asked.

"I can't imagine what. Her husband might think of some reason to blame her when things go wrong, and she'll think it's her fault. But it won't be."

"Why doesn't she leave?"

"And go where? She's in a wagon train in the middle of the country," Aunt Catherine said. "And when she gets to Colorado Territory, what could she do, take in washing?"

"Maybe she could travel with our wagon," I said.

"Pa wouldn't want that," Ma said. "He doesn't like to interfere with other people. That could cause trouble. He'd say it wasn't our business."

The two women were silent for a long time. Then Aunt Catherine said, "Remember what Mrs. Reid told us about sewing, that it helps with troubles? Well I don't think quilting will help her much."

More than anything I wanted there to be something that would help Mrs. Bonner.

Chapter Nine

GRANDMA MOUSE'S
SURPRISE

*W*hen Pa and Uncle Will returned, Ma told them she had loaned the hammer to Owen Bonner.

"That's the man who spoke up at the meeting, the one who said all the dogs ought to be shot or left behind," Uncle Will said. "And the cats, too."

I gasped, and thought about Skiddles. I'd never let anyone kill Skiddles. I thought Mr. Bonner was a bad man. He was mean to want to kill the dogs and cats, and he was mean to Mrs. Bonner, too.

"We voted him down," Pa said. "I didn't like him much. He seemed mighty impressed with himself."

"We didn't like him, either, and we've never met him," Ma said, "but his wife is a lovely person. She doesn't deserve to be treated in a despicable way."

"I suppose you'll get to know him later. Perhaps he's not so bad," Uncle Will said.

"We've already formed our opinion. It's not likely to change," Aunt Catherine told him.

"There are some nice people on this train, Meggie. I think you will make friends among them. Emmy Blue will, too," Pa said.

"It is a good train. Buttermilk John will be a fine scout," Uncle Will added. "He told us we can camp the way we are tonight, the wagons helter-skelter. But from tomorrow on, we will put them in a circle at night. That way, we'll be protected if Indians attack."

"Bonner protested, saying why go to that trouble before we reach Indian country, but John replied that if we are in the habit of forming a corral with the wagons, we can circle quickly if we need to. Besides, the animals and children will be safer inside the circle. There's less likelihood they'll run off—the animals or the children." Pa smiled at me.

It's too bad Mr. Bonner doesn't run off, I thought.

Buttermilk John had said we would leave not long after sunup each morning, taking turns at being the lead wagon, since with all the dust the oxen churned up, nobody wanted to be in the rear. But anyone who was not ready to go would have to take the last place.

After our breakfast the next morning, Pa and Uncle Will told us more about the meeting and the men who had attended it, while we returned the breakfast skillet and plates and forks to the wagon.

The men had discussed whether to stop to rest on Sundays. Many wanted to go on in order to get to Denver City as fast as they could, but Buttermilk John had told them that stopping one day each week would allow them to make repairs on their wagons. The women could bake and wash clothes, and the animals would rest. And in the long run, he said, the wagons that stopped for the Sabbath got there just as fast as the ones that went straight through. So, although Mr. Bonner and one or two others had grumbled, the rest of the wagon train had voted to declare Sunday a day of rest.

As we were repacking, Mrs. Bonner returned with the hammer—in two pieces. She could not look Ma in the eye but only muttered. "I am so sorry. Owen said the handle was defective, and it broke. I wish I could sneak into St. Joe and buy you a new one, but that is impossible. I promise I shall replace it once we reach Golden, if Owen will give me my money. After my escapade at the Patee House, Owen insisted that I let him hold on to the money I brought to our marriage, so that I would not be tempted to spend it."

Pa came up to Mrs. Bonner then and took the hammer.

Her head was down, and she stared at the ground. "I am sorry, sir. I never should have requested the loan of the implement. The fault is mine."

She wasn't at fault, I thought. It was her husband who had broken the hammer.

Since Pa knew about Mr. Bonner, he took the hammer pieces and said, "Most likely it was indeed defective."

As we watched Mrs. Bonner walk back to her wagon, Buttermilk John stepped forward. He had heard the conversation. "A hammer's defective if ye throw it against a rock the size of a bread loaf, which is what Bonner done, the blammity blam fool. This child seen him." He took the parts of the hammer from Pa. "Nail it back together. Then wrap the handle with wet buckskin, which'll shrink as it dries and turn hard as wood. I reckon your hammer will be as good as new then." Buttermilk John handed the hammer parts back to Pa and looked toward the Bonner wagon. Mr. Bonner was standing over his wife, who was stooped beside the campfire. "That one!" Buttermilk John said, shaking his head. "That one'll bear watching. He's worthless as a yellow dog."

That night we sat beside our fire, listening to the sounds of the camp. We had spent our days and nights by ourselves until we crossed the Missouri. Now instead of the noise of animals in the bushes and trees, we heard other people talking, laughing, children yelling. A woman at a campfire near us started to sing the hymn "A Mighty Fortress is Our God," and in a moment, others joined her. My voice isn't very good, but I sang, too. A man who had brought along a pump organ began to play.

After that song, the organist started "Camptown Races" and was joined by someone playing a mouth harp. We sang half a dozen songs before the women began calling to their children that it was time for bed.

As Aunt Catherine got up to fetch our blankets, Ma asked me, "Haven't you forgotten something, Emmy Blue?"

I jumped up. "I'll help," I said.

"No, not that. Have you forgotten we've crossed the Missouri River?"

I frowned, not knowing what she was talking about. How could I forget we had crossed the Missouri?

"Remember Grandma Mouse?"

"Of course I remember Grandma Mouse," I said. "I think about her every day. I miss her."

"Didn't she give you something? She said you could open it once we were across the Missouri."

And then I remembered the seed sack Grandma Mouse had given me the morning we left home. I reached into my pocket, but the sack wasn't there. "I don't have it," I said with a sad feeling.

"Maybe it's in the pocket of another dress," Ma said.

I reached into the pocket of my second dress. The seed sack wasn't there, either. But I changed the order in which I'd put on my dresses, wearing a different one on top each day. So I checked the third dress, and there was the seed sack! As I drew it out, I thought it might contain a book, but not a book like *The Girls' Own Book*, I hoped. I didn't want to read any more about good girls who helped in the kitchen and went right to bed, and bad girls who climbed trees and spilled their milk. If that kind of book was what was in the sack, I hoped Pa would say there wasn't room for it in the wagon. I wouldn't mind if she gave me an adventure book, although those were mostly for boys. Perhaps it was a jumping jack or marbles, but I realized the sack was the wrong size and weight for either of those things.

I unknotted the drawstring and opened the sack, turning it upside down so that the contents fell onto my skirt. Our campfire had gone out, and at first I couldn't see what Grandma had given me. I touched my lap and poked myself. "Ouch," I said, then felt around with the flat of my hand. I touched the object and held it up. "Scissors," I said, a dull feeling creeping into my heart. Then I felt an object, and without looking at it, I knew it was a thimble, a small thimble just the right size for my finger.

Something else had fallen out of the sack, but I didn't pick it up. Aunt Catherine leaned over and took the object. "A bundle of quilt pieces, already cut out," she said, holding them up to the light of the moon, which had just come out from behind a cloud. She laid them on top of the box that we used as a table, and then peered down at them in the moonlight. "Log Cabin, if I'm not mistaken. Look, Meggie, Grandma Mouse completed one of the blocks to use as a pattern. Isn't it cunning, just the right size for a doll's quilt?"

"Waxy already has a quilt that Abigail made for her," I said, trying not to sound disappointed. But I was. Who would think I wanted to make a quilt on our journey to Colorado Territory? Grandma Mouse, that was who. She was trying to turn me into a lady, and I wouldn't have it!

"Piecing on your own is much more fun than sitting under the table threading needles," Ma said.

Aunt Catherine laid out the pieces of one square on the box. "Grandma Mouse pinned together the pieces for each square, but I think you could change them. You don't have to do it her way. You could choose which pieces to put together. Your mother might even give you a scrap of the red calico we bought in St. Joe."

But it was still quilting, I thought. Even if Ma was a quilter, I didn't want to be one, not like Grandma Mouse.

"Look, Emmy Blue. See how the pieces fit together. They're like a puzzle. You like puzzles, don't you?"

I'd never thought of putting quilt pieces together as being like a puzzle, and I considered that, only slightly more interested now. I still wished Grandma Mouse had given me a book—a good book, one about a girl who ran foot races and played ball.

"We'll lay them out on the wagon seat in the morning," Aunt Catherine said. "At least you can fit them together. You won't have to sew them right away."

But I knew I would. If Grandma Mouse had given me the quilt pieces, Ma would surely make me stitch them together to form a quilt. I didn't understand why Ma loved quilting so much.

As I lay in my blankets that night, I knew why Grandmother had given me such a gift. It was because she wanted to turn me into a quilter. That wasn't much of a present, I decided. I might have to stitch those pieces together, but she'd never make a quilter out of me!

Chapter Ten

A PUZZLE WITHIN
A PUZZLE

*W*e left early in the morning, when Buttermilk John called out, "Wagons ho!" There were eighteen wagons, and half of them weren't ready. The rest of us scrambled for places in the front of the train, although Buttermilk John said it didn't matter who was first. We'd change places each day, the front wagon going to the back of the line and the rest of us moving up one place until we reached the front. That meant that each of us would be the lead wagon every eighteen days. The wagons that weren't ready hurried to catch up with us. Some didn't make it until our nooning.

We were number six in line, and the Bonner wagon was behind us. Ma told Aunt Catherine, whose wagon was in front of ours, that we'd be able to keep an eye on Mrs. Bonner.

"She will need friends," Ma said.

With all the commotion and the excitement, Ma forgot about Grandma Mouse's quilt pieces, which was fine with me. At first I sat beside her on the wagon, but the seat was hard, and there was nothing to do but look at the backsides of the oxen in front of us. So after a time, when the oxen stopped for a moment, I jumped down and walked alongside Pa.

"What do you think of the wagon train, Emmy Blue?" he asked.

"I like it." And I did. There were people and dogs and all kinds of prairie schooners. Some were well made and grand like ours. Others were rickety. One driver had already fallen out of line to fix a wobbly wheel. I liked the noise of the oxen and mules, and of the cowbells that clanked as milk cows were herded along beside the wagons. People yelled and laughed. Men shouted at the animals. One woman sang to a baby she held in her arms. I especially liked the sound of children calling, because I had been the only child from the time we left home until we crossed the Missouri.

As I walked along beside Pa, I studied the other children. There were plenty of little ones who were too young for me, and half a dozen who were almost grown, too old to want to play. I looked for a girl my size, someone like Abigail, who could be my friend. But I didn't see anyone. Then I spotted a boy who was two wagons in front of us. He seemed about my age. He was smaller than me, and he had freckles all over his face. Like me, he was barefoot. He must have been going barefoot for a long time, because walking over the stones on the trail didn't seem to bother his feet. I'd worn shoes until we reached the Missouri, and my feet weren't hardened yet. I crept along, trying to avoid rocks and sharp sticks.

"See that young'un up there," Pa said, as if he knew I was staring at the boy. "He's Joey Schmidt. His father's German. Mr. Schmidt is a baker, and he wants to open a confectionary shop in Colorado. His wagon's loaded to the gills with pans and flour and spices to make breads and cake. I thought I might see if he'd like to set up shop in a fine business block in Golden. What would you say to that, Emmy Blue? Pies and cakes in our building!"

I grinned at Pa to show him that was a good idea.

"Joey Schmidt's just about your age. His father says he's shy. Why don't you make friends with him?"

I shrugged and dragged my big toe in the dirt, but deep down I thought it was a good idea.

"Go on, Emmy Blue. He's a nice boy, and I expect he's lonely for the company of other children, just like you are." Pa gave me a gentle shove, so I didn't have much choice. I walked toward the Schmidt wagon, turning once to look at Pa, who waved me on. Finally I reached Joey Schmidt. "Hi," I said, not looking at Joey.

"Hi yourself," he said. He didn't seem so shy.

"Pa says you're my age."

"I'm eight."

I made a face. Eight was awfully young. "Well, I'm ten."

"I'll be nine in twenty-seven days. Papa says he'll make a layer cake for my birthday. If you're my friend, you can have some."

Except for the cakes Aunt Catherine had bought at the Patee House in St. Joseph, we hadn't had sweets since the first week of our trip, and my mouth watered. "How's your pa going to bake a cake on the trail?"

"He's pretty good. He will bake the cake in the coals of a campfire."

"What about frosting?"

"Whipped cream."

I licked my lips. "How can he do that?"

"We brought our cow with us."

"I guess I could be your friend," I said.

Joey nodded. "I brought my sack of marbles. Do you know how to play?" He looked at me skeptically.

"Sure."

"You're a girl. Girls play with dolls. And they sew."

"I don't sew, unless I have to." Then I added, "My friend Betsy taught me to play marbles, but I didn't bring any. There wasn't room in the wagon."

"For marbles? They don't take up any room."

I shrugged. "There wasn't room for our clothes either."

"Is that why you're dressed funny, with all those dresses?" I nodded.

"Our wagon's filled with stuff so Papa can set up a bakery. Mama had to leave her rocking chair behind."

"So did my ma." I decided I liked Joey. We had something in common. "Pa says you're German."

"No, Papa is, but me and Mama are one hundred percent Americans. I don't even sound like a German. You want to shoot marbles? You can use mine."

"Really?"

"Sure." Joey called up to his mother. "Mama, will you throw me down my sack of marbles?"

"You be careful, Joseph. Don't lose them. And you keep up with the train. We don't want to lose you, neither." She glanced at me and added, "Be sure you count them marbles when you're done."

I had just met Mrs. Schmidt, and already I didn't like her.

"She worries all the time," Joey said to me. "She thinks an Indian's going to snatch me up, or a bear, even though Papa says there aren't any bears on the prairie. I'm all they've got, you see. My sister died of the whooping cough last year, and my brother was run over by a wagon soon after that."

I understood. I was my parents' only living child, too. Sometimes that was a burden.

Joey and I found a flat, hard place just off the trail, and he opened the sack and let the marbles fall to the ground.

"That's my best marble, my shooter," he said, picking up one that was black with a white spot on it. "You can use the next best." He pointed to a red one.

As I reached for it, our wagon passed, and Pa called, "Don't fall too far behind, Emmy Blue."

I barely paid Pa any attention, because Joey was down on one knee, his black-and-white marble in his hand. He was good. If I'd had my own marbles with me, he'd have won most of them. But after a time, I got comfortable shooting, and I won some of the marbles. Of course, they weren't mine to keep. Joey had only loaned them to me. We played until the last wagon passed. Then we picked up the marbles and ran to catch up. "Did you count them?" I asked, remembering Joey's mother.

"Nah. I trust you. Do you want to play tomorrow?" Joey asked as I stopped beside Pa. "We can play something besides marbles, if you got anything."

But all I had was Waxy—and those darn quilt pieces. No boy would want to sit on a wagon seat and stitch. "No," I told him. "I don't have anything to play with."

After our nooning, and when we were on the trail again, Ma took out the seed sack, which she had tucked into a side pocket of the wagon. She put the square Grandma Mouse had completed on the wagon seat, then unpinned one of the bunches of tiny quilt pieces that Grandma Mouse had cut out. I had already counted the bundles. There were fourteen of them, fifteen if you counted the one Grandma Mouse had already made. And when they were finished, the squares had to be stitched together.

"Aunt Catherine is right. This is a Log Cabin pattern. Grandma Mouse made it small, just the right size for Waxy. Wasn't that clever of her?"

"Yes, ma'am," I replied, thinking Grandma Mouse was clever all right. Because of her, I was stuck with making a quilt!

Ma laid out the pieces of a single quilt square on the wagon seat, sixteen strips and a bright red square. "Now, we'll figure out just how they fit together. The red square always goes in the center, because red stands for the hearth, which is the center of any home," she explained. "Now, find the smallest piece and lay it beside the square."

I went through the tiny strips until I found one that was white with light green flowers in it and laid it next to the square.

"Good. Now the next smallest one."

I found a blue strip and laid it across the ends of the red square and the white piece, but it was too long. I looked through the pieces until I came across another white strip, this one with blue dots. It was the perfect length for the other two.

"You see, you're circling around the red square."

A dust devil blew up and lifted one of the quilt pieces, and I made a grab for it before I thought I should have let it blow away and be trampled in the road. That would have meant one less quilt square to make. But then I realized Ma would have used her own fabric to cut a strip to replace the missing piece.

Ma put the scissors down on the quilt pieces that we had laid out so the wind wouldn't catch them. "What about the next piece, Emmy Blue?" she asked.

I searched through the strips and picked out a plain dark blue strip of calico. And then, without Ma asking, I picked the next piece, a brown with black flowers, and finished off the square. I frowned at the pieces of material I'd laid out. "How come the first two are light and the next two are dark?" I asked.

"It's part of the pattern, the darks on one side, the lights on the other. When you join the quilt squares together, you'll lay them out in such a way that the darks and lights form a pattern themselves. A Log Cabin quilt is a puzzle within a puzzle."

But not a very good one, I thought. Who wanted to put together fourteen puzzles that were just the same, and stitch them at that? I started to stuff the pieces into the sack, but Ma put out her hand. "Not so fast, Emmy Blue. Grandma Mouse gave this to you so that you could quilt on the way to Colorado Territory. It would be ungracious of you not to do as she wants. You don't have to sit all day and quilt. I know that would tax you. But I expect you to make a full circle of quilt strips each day. That means today you will start out by sewing four pieces around the red center. Tomorrow you can make a second circle of pieces. Why, in four days, you'll have completed one square. So your quilt top will be done before we reach Golden."

"Will you help me?" I asked. Ma was so fast she could be done with all fourteen squares before I finished one.

But Ma saw what I was up to and gave me a smile. "I will check that each one is done properly, else it will have to be taken out and re-stitched the next day. But I won't do the stitching myself. There're many women out there who would refuse to have another woman take a single stitch in her quilt."

"Not me."

Ma laughed at that. "No, not you, but in time."

I turned away, because I wanted to get down from the wagon and find Joey. He didn't have to sit on the seat and sew. Ma grabbed my dress. "The best time to start is now, Emmy Blue."

Ma was firm. So I sighed to show her I was not happy. She took out a threaded needle that was pinned to the under-side of her collar—she kept it there so that she could sew whenever she could—and handed it to me. "You can sit beside me on the wagon seat and work."

"Or you can quilt as you walk along," Aunt Catherine said as she walked up beside us. She explained she was tired of sitting and had come to see if Ma wanted to walk with her. Aunt Catherine changed her mind about asking Ma when she saw the pieces of fabric spread out on the wagon seat. "You come with me, Emmy Blue. I have my sewing and you can bring yours. We'll take a quilt walk."

"Yes, ma'am," I said, glancing ahead at Joey's wagon. I'd told him I didn't sew unless I had to, so I didn't want him to see me on any quilt walk.

Chapter Eleven

PA DOES MR. BONNER'S WORK

$\mathcal{I}$ finished the first quilt square in three days! It was not because I liked quilting, of course. I knew that the faster I stitched, the sooner the quilt would be done and I could think about other things. So I stitched as I walked along, sometimes with Aunt Catherine, sometimes alone. I even stitched with Joey, who didn't seem to mind that I was sewing. The piecing went quicker than I'd thought—too fast, Ma said one evening as she examined the quilt square by the light of our campfire.

"Look at this, Emmy Blue. These stitches are much too large and uneven to be acceptable, and you've sewn too close to the edge of the material. If I allow you to keep in the stitches, the fabric will unravel and you'll have an unsightly seam. You must take them out."

"But it's only a doll's quilt. Waxy isn't hard on her quilts. She won't know the difference."

"I will, and so will you. You must do them over."

"But, Ma."

"No." Ma's tone was serious. "If you don't learn to stitch correctly now, you never will, and your quilts will be an embarrassment. There is nothing so unattractive as a woman with sloppy habits. Take out the stitches on these last four pieces and sew them properly."

I turned to Aunt Catherine to back me up, but she only smiled and said Ma was right, that if a thing was worth doing, it was worth doing right.

I wanted to say I didn't think quilting was worth doing at all, but I knew Ma would tell me I was brash. So I took the little scissors Grandma Mouse had given me and clipped out the bad stitches, setting me back half a day. Since I didn't want to lose that time, I sat beside the fire and re-stitched the four quilt pieces before I went to bed. When I was finished, Ma looked at the work and nodded her approval, then ironed the seams to one side with her fingers.

After that, I stitched one circle of four pieces while I was sitting on the wagon seat, another on a quilt walk with Aunt Catherine and another while I sat beside the campfire after dinner. That way, the quilt would be finished three times as fast, and I would be done with it.

- - - - - - - - -

Traveling in a wagon train was different from making the journey on our own. Our oxen and wagon were dirty because of the dust churned up by seventeen other Conestogas. It was noisy, too, with the din of oxen and horses and mules, drivers yelling, children screaming, cowbells clanging. Not that I minded.

The countryside changed after we crossed the Missouri River. I was used to grassy meadows, but now there was open prairie. Pa called the farms hardscrabble. The people living on them were poor and thin. They stared at us as we passed, sometimes raising an arm to wave but not smiling. "I bet nothing will ever hatch out of that farm," Pa said, as we passed one field. Many times we camped on the dusty prairie, far from a stream. As water became scarce we had to be careful not to waste it.

The cakes and pies and stews that our neighbors had given us had been eaten long before we crossed the Missouri. And there weren't any farmers to sell us fresh vegetables and dairy products now. Instead we ate prairie chicken that Pa shot, beans and bacon, slapjacks with black molasses, stewed peaches, ham biscuits, and cornbread that Ma and Aunt Catherine made on Sundays. Sunday was baking day, and Ma always made a dried apple pie. We liked dried apple pie, though Pa said we were liable to get tired of it by the time we reached Golden. He said some travelers were so sick of

dried apples that they made up a song about them, and he
taught it to me:

> *I loathe, abhor, detest, despise,*
> *Abominate dried apple pies.*
> *I like good bread, I like good meat*
> *Or anything that's good to eat.*
> *But of all the poor grub beneath the skies,*
> *The poorest is dried apple pies.*
> *So give me the toothache or sore eyes*
> *But don't give me dried apple pies.*
> *Tread on my corns or tell me lies,*
> *But don't pass me dried apple pies!*

Our food was *plains* fare, Ma said, because the prairie we
crossed was known as the Great Plains. I didn't complain
about the monotony of our meals, because I saw that everyone in the wagon train ate the same food, and some were less
fortunate than we were, living on just beans and bacon, with
never a taste of pie or gingerbread or even stewed apples or
peaches.

Only the Schmidts ate better than we did. On Sundays,
Mr. Schmidt baked a cake in a cast-iron Dutch oven and
sometimes he made cookies with black walnuts, too. Joey
shared the desserts with me, until Mrs. Schmidt called me a
poor little beggar girl. After that, I told Joey I wasn't hungry.

"Oh, don't mind Ma. She's homesick," he said. I could tell he was embarrassed at the way his mother treated me.

I didn't change my mind about Mrs. Schmidt, though. She complained all the time, telling her husband that he was a fool to sell their bakeshop and go west. She said Joey would grow up to be a wild Indian, that is, if he didn't get himself trampled by a buffalo first. "And what about me?" I overheard her ask. "What will happen to me if you get shot in the head by an Indian or run over by a stupid ox? What will happen to me and Joey if you're not around to take care of us?" And then I heard her mutter, "I should have married the hardware clerk, but I was a fool for sweet strawberry tarts."

Mrs. Schmidt complained about the land we passed through, but Joey and I were fascinated by it. We discovered rocks that were smooth and black as night, and broken stones that gleamed as if they contained gold. I asked Pa about them, but he said they were just rocks. We picked up a snakeskin, flowers I'd never seen before, feathers, and eggshells. Ma told me that every Sunday I could choose one item and store it in a small drawer in the medicine chest that she had discovered was empty. Already it contained a speckled shell, brown with tiny dots of black and white. There were also two rocks, the red one so soft I could write with it, and the white one with the outline of a fern. There was a scarlet leaf and a dried flower. Ma called the flower a lady's slipper, and said she did not know how it could have grown in that dry earth. I found a tiny green bead, like the ones on Buttermilk John's shirt, and told Ma that an Indian must have left it for me. But Ma said it was more likely that it was lost by one of the travelers. Once, I discovered the arm of a china doll under a bush and added that to the collection, thinking how unhappy the doll's owner would be when she discovered the arm had broken off. I wished she could know that it was safe in our medicine chest.

There was a little more room in the wagon, now that part of our food supply was gone, and I asked Ma, "Couldn't we store some of our clothes in the wagon? Do we have to keep on wearing them all?"

Ma glanced at Aunt Catherine and didn't answer me right away.

"Your ma's proud," Aunt Catherine said.

"I want to show your pa I will live up to my promise," Ma said. Then to show the subject was closed, she added, "Let me see your quilt square, Emmy Blue."

Only a couple of weeks after we left the Missouri, we began to pass dead animals, oxen and mules that had given out, sometimes a dog that had been run over by a wagon. I knew then that Pa had been right when he'd insisted I leave Skiddles behind. I wouldn't have wanted my cat to be crushed under an oak wheel or attacked by one of the big dogs the settlers had brought along.

Then I realized that animals weren't all that perished crossing the plains, because we spotted our first grave, a pile of stones with a crude wooden marker. The grave was new, I could tell, but the words painted on the marker had already begun to fade, and all we could read was "Alb rt K ne."

"A man," Pa said, when we stopped the wagon to see the grave. "I wonder what happened to him."

"Or a boy," Ma replied.

I thought then of Agnes Ruth, my little sister who had died, and wondered if Ma was remembering her and the other graves we had left behind in Quincy.

"It might have been a woman—Alberta," Aunt Catherine put in. "Perhaps she had young children. Who would take care of them?"

"Others in the train. There are always mothers to take on the young." Ma glanced my way as if to reassure me that if something happened to her, I would not be alone.

Ma's words made me worry that one of them might get hurt or even killed. If something happened to Pa, would Ma and I be able to drive the oxen by ourselves? But then, would Ma and I even continue to Colorado Territory on our own?

What if it was Ma who got hurt or died, what would become of us? I wasn't the only one who would be lost without her. What would Pa be like without Ma? She had the stouter heart.

Then I thought, what would happen to me if both of them died? Would Uncle Will and Aunt Catherine want me? Ma, Pa, Aunt Catherine, and Uncle Will were the people I loved most in the world. I couldn't bear it if one of them were killed or even hurt in any way, and if something happened to all of them, I'd have to go back to Quincy and hope Abigail and her mother would take me in.

Suppose I was the one to get hurt, what would they do? They needed me. I ran back and forth between the wagons with messages. I took Pa's place beside the oxen when he had some chore to do. If something happened to me, would I be buried like Alb rt K ne, left under a pile of rocks, remembered for only a few weeks until my name bleached away in the sun? Would Ma and Pa go on without me?

"Do you think anybody will remember whoever's buried here?" I asked.

"We will remember," Aunt Catherine said. She had gathered a bouquet of grasses and wildflowers, and now she put them on the stones covering the grave.

I'll remember, too, I thought.

The Bonner wagon had pulled out behind us. Mr. Bonner said one of his wheels was not right and he wanted to check it.

"Hatchett," he called. "Give me a hand."

Pa and Uncle Will looked at each other. Because they were brothers, both of them were named Hatchett. I wondered if each expected the other to help Mr. Bonner, but in the end, both went to him.

Mr. Bonner told his wife, "Well, get down off the seat. If we have to lift the wagon, we don't want you in it."

Even from where I stood, I could see Mrs. Bonner's face turn red, and she jumped off the wagon and came to stand beside us. "The wheel plagues him," she explained to Ma.

"Made by a scoundrel," Mr. Bonner added in a loud voice.

Serves him right, I thought.

Mrs. Bonner spotted the grave. "Oh, how awful! To think of dying in this lonely place and buried far from loved ones."

"We'll see more graves before our journey's over," Aunt Catherine said. "Pray God it won't be one of us."

"I couldn't bear to be left behind like that," Mrs. Bonner said. Then she glanced at her husband and rubbed her wrist, which looked bruised. I could see her lip was split, too. "But I wonder if there are worse things than dying," she added quietly. "And it would be peaceful, lying under the sod with only the wind to trouble one. I think it might not be such a bad fate at that."

"There would be wildflowers, too," I said. I had my quilt square in my hand, and I held it up to show her a strip with yellow flowers on it.

"Yes, I'd like that, to lie under a carpet of flowers. I believe I like flowers best of all God's creations," Mrs. Bonner told us. "Owen said in one of his letters before we were married that he loved roses, but I believe he loves the thorns better than the blossoms." She put her hand to her mouth and lowered her head, as if she should not have spoken. "I must watch what I say. I am so used to speaking my mind. Owen says a tongue is a bad thing in a woman, and I fear he may be right." She gave an odd laugh, one that told me she was scared. "Listen to me prattle on. Owen is right to teach me my place."

"He is a handsome man," Ma said at last. Ma rarely commented on people's looks, because she said what was inside a person was more important. So when Ma said that Mr. Bonner was handsome, I knew she couldn't think of anything else nice to say about him.

"Yes, isn't he?" Mrs. Bonner replied. "My friends considered me a lucky woman to have made such a good marriage. And to think I met him through the letters. I could scarce believe my good fortune when I first saw him." She leaned forward as if sharing a secret. "I had worried he would be an ugly man."

"And it was his good fortune to find a beautiful wife," Aunt Catherine said.

Mrs. Bonner shook her head. "I am plain. Even Owen

says so. I fear he was disappointed."

"Plain? Not at all! Why your face is like a doll's."

"Like Waxy's, before she sat in the sun," I added. Mrs. Bonner looked confused, until I explained that Waxy was my wax doll, whose face had softened from the sun's heat.

"Not so fine, but at least I will not melt," Mrs. Bonner said with a small smile. She looked at the quilt square I was stitching. "I wish I had brought my sewing with me. It would be an excellent thing to sit in the sun with it while we rest."

"Do you quilt?" Ma asked.

"Oh yes. And if you will excuse my vanity, I was considered quite good at it in Fort Madison. But I am speaking about embroidery. It is my favorite, and I am afraid I am too proud of it. You see, I embroidered the pillow slips and sheets, the towels and tablecloths for my wedding trip, and I decorate my under things. She took a handkerchief from her pocket and showed it to us. The white linen square was embroidered with white flowers, and there was fine lace around the edges.

"Such delicate stitches. Why, there's not a single mistake," Ma said admiringly. "I am hoping Emmy Blue will learn to stitch as well." She nodded her head at my quilt square.

For fear Ma would suggest I learn to embroider, too, I went over to where the men were working on the wheel. A spoke had split, and Pa was telling Mr. Bonner about wrapping it in wet buckskin.

"Never heard of that, but I guess there's no harm in you doing it," Mr. Bonner said.

Pa glanced at Uncle Will in a way that told me I knew he was angry. "Me?" he muttered. Mr. Bonner made no move to fix the spoke, so Pa went to our wagon, found a piece of buckskin, and whittled off a strip with his knife. He poured water over it, working the wetness into the buckskin, and when it was pliable, he stretched it, and then wound it around the spoke.

Ma saw that Pa was doing all the work. But she didn't say anything. Instead, she removed her sunbonnet and examined it. "Worn out already," she said, running her hand over the fabric. "I was vain and made it from fine muslin. I should have used calico, and a dark one so the dirt wouldn't show. But it will have to do now."

"I'll make you a new one if you don't mind," Mrs. Bonner said quickly.

Ma shook her head. "I ought to make my own, to punish myself for my vanity."

"But I should love to do it for you. You have been such good neighbors to Owen and me. And I would enjoy a change from the embroidery. I even have the fabric for a sunbonnet, a dark blue that would flatter your eyes. Please allow me."

At home, Ma would never have let anyone do her sewing for her, and I was afraid she might think Mrs. Bonner's work wasn't up to her standards. But I could tell that Mrs. Bonner was trying to be nice, because her husband was not. He'd broken our hammer, and now he was letting Pa mend the wheel.

"I wouldn't want to put you to the trouble," Ma said at last, and I knew Mrs. Bonner had won.

"No trouble at all. I'd welcome the work."

The wagon wheel was mended and Mr. Bonner yelled to his wife to stop gabbing and get into the wagon. He helped Mrs. Bonner onto the seat, but maybe that was because we were watching him.

"I do not care much for that man," Ma said when Pa and Uncle Will joined us. "Did he even thank you?"

Pa shrugged. "It's a rickety wagon, and he's too lazy to grease the hubs. I'll wager this won't be the only time something goes wrong with it."

"Well, I hope that next time, you're not there to help him," Ma said.

"I was just being neighborly."

"Yes, you were. And we had a chance to visit with Mrs. Bonner. I imagine she needs women to talk to. I suspect he lays the weight of his hand on her, and she's harmless as a dove. Couldn't you say something to Mr. Bonner, Thomas?"

"It's not our business. Besides, he's not a man that bears talking to," Pa replied.

I wondered whether Pa would think Mr. Bonner would bear talking to if he hurt Ma—or me.

Chapter Twelve

FIRST IN LINE

❊

*N*ot long after that, we began to come across posses-
sions that travelers had discarded along the trail. Of course,
all along we'd seen things that had been thrown out—broken
dishes, ripped clothing, and the like. But now we spotted
more valuable items. Ma called them "leavings." One was
a large chair made of polished wood with gilt trim on the
edges. The chair was upholstered in yellow silk with a pattern
of bees on it.

"Stop, Thomas," Ma called when she saw it. She climbed
down from the wagon and made her way to the chair. "It's
been so long since I sat in a real chair that I can't resist trying
it out." She ran the back of her hand over the arm, and with
a contented sigh she settled into it. She leaned her head back

and closed her eyes. "Feel the silk, Emmy Blue," she said. "It's so fine I have to use the backs of my hands to touch it for fear of snagging it." Then she laughed. "Listen to me. I suppose my hands aren't any rougher than the sand and wind that will destroy this upholstery in a day. Why a single raindrop would leave a mark."

Aunt Catherine walked over to us. "This is finer than anything I had at home. The woman who owned this chair must have cried when she parted with it. Still, I wonder at taking along such a silly piece of furniture in the first place."

Ma stood up. "You sit, Cath, and you will understand. It must have meant to her what my rocker did to me." They traded places, and Aunt Catherine took her turn in the chair, resting her arms on the yellow silk.

After she stood up, I slipped into the chair and snuggled into the down of the cushion. I sat there as long as I could, thinking I could sleep in that chair. It certainly was softer than the ground.

But Pa said, "Come along, Emmy Blue." Ma was already back on the wagon seat, and Pa was flicking his whip at the oxen. I had to hurry to catch up.

"It's a pretty chair," I told him, as I walked along beside Pa. "Why would somebody leave it behind?"

"To lighten their load. Oxen are strong, but even they have a limit. We'll come across more useless belongings before we get to Golden."

And we did. We passed washstands and bureaus, kitchen chairs and love seats, bedsteads, stoves, and even a sewing machine.

Once, we stopped beside a pile of bedding—blankets and pillow slips, sheets and quilts. The quilts were neatly folded, and on top was a note held down by a rock. Ma picked it up and read, "Help yourself to six good quilts." She turned to Aunt Catherine. "She must have felt as if she were leaving behind her right arm."

The two of them went through the coverlets. "Look at the star quilt. The corners are perfect," Aunt Catherine said.

"I prefer a star to all other patterns," Ma said. "Maybe that's why I enjoy sleeping under the starry sky at night. Can you see the stitches, Emmy Blue? They're as fine as grains of sand. Just imagine the quilter's heartache at parting with them!"

The two looked at the quilts, then folded them and placed the note and the rock back on top of them. "If we just had a place, I would take the star," Ma said.

"But you don't," Aunt Catherine reminded her. "If you took the quilt, then Thomas would make you throw out your own Friendship Quilt. I don't have room, either. Surely some woman will have a place in her prairie schooner."

As we walked back to the wagons, a man stopped to look through the discarded items. He held up a red, white, and blue quilt with stars and stripes and remarked, "This will do for a saddle blanket. I'll just tear it in half." He went through the quilts again and took out a second one. "This will go on top of the wagon sheet to keep out the rain."

Ma looked at Aunt Catherine and shook her head. "God forbid the maker ever learns what happened to her handiwork."

"No need to worry. That man's a go-back," Aunt Catherine said. We watched as he placed the quilts in his wagon and started off to the east.

We'd passed go-backs before, single men and families who had given up finding a fortune and were returning home. Some turned around even before they reached Colorado Territory, but others had been all the way to the mountains. When they hadn't found gold, they were too discouraged to stay. Many of the travelers had painted "Pike's Peak or Bust" on their wagon sheets before they left home. The go-backs had crossed out those words and written "Busted by Golly" underneath.

As we watched the man drive his wagon away, I asked Ma if she wanted to go back home, too. She thought about that for a long time and didn't answer. Instead, she said, "I like the sky here that is so blue and clear, and the open space. It seems as if you can see a hundred miles." Then she paused and added, "But I'll always miss Grandpa Bluestone, Grandma Mouse, and my friends. I wonder if I shall ever have such true friends again."

"You have Aunt Catherine," I reminded her.

"I do, and I have you, Emmy Blue. Now why should I want for more?"

Pa and Uncle Will had gone ahead with the wagons, and Ma, Aunt Catherine, and I walked together, the three of us in a row, through the prairie grass. The animals churned up so much dust that we didn't want to follow behind them on the trail.

"How is your quilting coming, Emmy Blue?" Aunt Catherine asked.

I shrugged, thinking that it wasn't coming fast enough. I hoped this didn't turn into a quilt-walk day.

"Show her your square," Ma suggested.

I took it out of my pocket, pressing it against my hand to get out the wrinkles. Then I held it up. But I sighed as I did so, because I had used a dark strip where I should have used a light one. "I guess I have to take that one out," I said, before Ma could tell me I was sloppy.

Ma took the square from me and studied it. "Oh, leave it be," she said to my surprise. "Only God is perfect. You don't have to be."

I opened my mouth so wide at her remark that you could have tossed an apple down my throat without touching my tongue.

"Do you know that Bessie Fisk at home purposely made a mistake in each of her quilts?" Aunt Catherine said. "She told me she thought God would be offended if she made a perfect quilt."

"Well, she didn't have to trouble herself. She makes enough mistakes for all of us," Ma said. She and Aunt Catherine began to giggle.

"Meggie, shame on you," Aunt Catherine said, and laughed again. Then she took my quilt square from Ma and studied it. "One piece put in like that will only add interest to your quilt, Emmy Blue. Why, some might even think you did it on purpose. I would be one of them."

I wouldn't, but I didn't say so.

A drop of rain fell onto the quilt square, and Aunt Catherine looked up at the sky. "Hurry along, Meggie. We mustn't lag too far behind. The weather is about to turn. I believe we are in for a real rain."

The sky was turning dark, and the air was suddenly cold. When I looked up, drops of rain fell onto my face. We hurried along, and by the time we reached our wagons, the sky had opened up. Ma and I huddled together on the wagon seat, wrapped in a quilt that was covered by an oilskin poncho. But still we got wet. I hoped Buttermilk John would call a halt so that we could set up our tent, but I knew he wouldn't. He'd said we wouldn't stop for anything but a presidential election. I asked what that meant, and Ma explained that we wouldn't stop for anything at all, since the presidential election wasn't until fall, long after we expected to reach Colorado Territory. "Your Pa will vote for Mr. Abraham Lincoln," she added.

So we sat huddled on the wagon seat in the heavy, cold rain, our wet sunbonnets limp around our faces.

At last, Buttermilk John decided on a camping spot, and we climbed down from the wagon. The prairie had turned to what he called gumbo. I could feel the mud squeeze between my toes, since like the other children in the wagon train, I went barefoot to save my shoes.

We usually slept under the wagon or out in the open, but with the storm, Pa got out the tent, which was just a canvas cover supported by four poles. Then Ma and Aunt Catherine spread an India rubber cloth on the ground to keep our bedding dry. Usually Uncle Will and Aunt Catherine slept apart from us, but that night we all crowded together under the awning.

With the rain coming down so hard, Ma couldn't build a campfire. "We'll have to make do with cold biscuits and last night's beans—and water instead of coffee, plenty of water," Ma said. "It's a poor supper, but we'll fill up in the morning with slapjacks and bacon. That is, if it stops raining. I never knew such a miserable day."

Lightning split the sky. Ma watched it, then turned to me.

"Did you see that, Emmy Blue? The pattern in your quilt pieces will zigzag like that when you put them together."

I didn't like to be reminded of the quilt, because with the rain, I hadn't stitched on it all day and would have to do twice as much work tomorrow to keep up. If the rain stopped, tomorrow would be a quilt-walk day for sure.

Huddled together that night, we slept well. Although the wind blew raindrops onto the quilts that covered us, we were dry because the India rubber cloth kept out the dampness from the earth. By morning, the rain was gone, and the air was clear. The sun was bright. Ma said it made the drops of water clinging to the grass shine as if they were the diamonds in Aunt Catherine's ring. And the wildflowers that came after the rain were the colors of the bright strips of fabric in the quilt top I was piecing.

The ground was still muddy, but instead of complaining about it, Ma rubbed her arms and said, "My skin was so dry from the sun yesterday. Now it has moisture in it."

"We'll have to drive through this muck until the ground dries out, but it shouldn't take long with the sun shining," Pa said. He was knocking yesterday's mud off the wagon wheels.

"At least we won't have dust," Ma said. She had set out our skillet and kettle as well as our water barrel the night before to collect rainwater. We usually filled up the barrel when we crossed a stream, but the water there was sometimes muddy from where the animals and wagons had churned it. Now we had fresh, clear water.

We were the lead wagon that day, and Pa hurried to hitch up the oxen so that we would be ready to go before Buttermilk John cried, "Move 'em out." But as we were waiting to start, Mr. Bonner pulled his wagon in front of us. When Pa protested, Mr. Bonner said, "I believe I was afore you yesterday."

It was true. The day before, Mr. Bonner had yelled to Pa that his wagon sheet had come loose in the wind and rain, so we'd pulled out of line to help him. But as it turned out, the cover was firmly attached, and Mr. Bonner had pushed ahead of us. It was late in the day, and Pa hadn't said anything.

Now Pa looked at Ma before he replied. Ma didn't like confrontations, and usually said to let things be. But she had a determined look on her face now, just like Pa, and she nodded once.

"That was before you crowded in," Pa told Mr. Bonner.

"You telling me this ain't my place?" Mr. Bonner had a mean look on his face.

"I'm telling you I'm in the lead today. Your place is behind me," Pa said.

Ma clutched my hand, and I was sorry Uncle Will and Aunt Catherine weren't close by. They had been the lead wagon the day before, so now it was their turn to bring up the rear. They were all the way at the end of the line of wagons.

"I say I'm in the lead, and I'm staying here, 'less you want to fight me for it," Mr. Bonner shouted.

"Owen," Mrs. Bonner said, so softly I could barely hear her. "I'm afraid Mr. Hatchett is right. Our position is behind him."

"Be still!" he yelled at her. "Don't you know when to be still? You got no business speaking against your husband. You hear me?"

Mrs. Bonner looked down at her hands and said nothing.

"Never would I have a thing to do with that man if it wasn't for his wife!" Ma said under her breath. "Lord forgive me, but I shouldn't mind if he got trampled by his own oxen. And the way he hits the poor animals, he just might." Ma turned to me. "Emmy Blue, it's time you learned there are some things a woman shouldn't have to abide by, and that man is one of them."

"I said, get behind me, Bonner," Pa said. He didn't yell. In fact, I had to strain to hear him. But there was anger in his voice that I had heard only two or three times in my life, once when a man was beating a dog. Pa's eyes were hard, and he stood with his feet apart, his fist clinched. Because Pa limped, some men might have thought he was weak. Not Pa! I knew he could whip Mr. Bonner. I'd never seen Pa fight, but I'd heard Grandma Mouse say that when he was younger, Pa was a good man with his fists.

Mr. Bonner held his whip in one hand while he seemed to size up Pa. I didn't take my eyes off Mr. Bonner, but out of the corner of my eye I saw that other men had stopped what they were doing and were watching. Two of them had left their wagons and went to stand behind Pa. Mr. Bonner shifted from one foot to the other, his eyes darting from one man to another. It looked like he wasn't sure what to do.

Slowly, Pa reached for his own whip, which was on the wagon seat. At first, I was afraid he would strike Mr. Bonner with it, but instead, he tapped it on the rump of our lead ox and said, "Giddup." Our wagon swung out into the lead position. After a time, Mr. Bonner pulled his wagon in behind us. The others went back to their wagons, nodding their approval, and a few minutes later, Buttermilk John rode up to Pa and said, "Ye be smart about that, old son."

I was still shaking a little bit as I walked beside Pa. "Why didn't you fight Mr. Bonner?" I asked. "You could have beat him easy," I said. "It would show him right."

"Maybe so, Emmy Blue, but that would have made him even madder than he already is. He'd take it out on us in some way, and maybe on Mrs. Bonner, too. You have to stand your ground, but there's no reason to rile folks unless you have to."

"I bet he fights dirty," I said.

"That's a bet you'd win. Just look at his wife."

"Why does he hit her?"

Pa thought that over. "Some men are just no good."

"Can't you do something about it?"

"I don't believe it's my place to interfere between a man and his wife." He paused. "But I have a feeling your ma doesn't agree with me on that."

I didn't agree with him, either.

Chapter Thirteen

HURRAH FOR SURPRISE

❖

We had gone only a little ways when Buttermilk John came up to our wagon. "There's animals got loose in last night's storm. A few of us are going after them. We'd be obliged if ye'd be one. I got a horse for ye to ride."

Pa looked at Ma and asked, "Can you lead the team without me?"

"Of course," Ma replied. "I have Emmy Blue to help me." Ma had walked beside the oxen before when Pa went hunting, so it wouldn't be the first time she and I had been alone with the team.

"We won't be gone long," Pa said. "The trail's almost dry now. And the oxen will be easy, now that they've had water to drink." He glanced at me and grinned. "I believe Emmy

Blue could handle the team on her own, if she had to."

"We'll be all right," Ma said.

Pa turned to look at Mr. Bonner behind us. "If he gives you any trouble, just raise your voice. He's a coward. I don't want to leave you, but the folks in the train are our neighbors. It'll be hard-going for them if they've lost some of their oxen. "They'll have to lighten their wagons. They might even have to throw out their quilts."

He smiled at his joke, but Ma didn't. Pa'd made her discard some of her quilts before we even left Quincy, and I knew she hadn't forgot that.

Ma, too, had a hard time turning down anyone in need, which Pa knew, and she said, "Go along, Thomas."

"You're a good woman, Meggie." He cleared his throat. "We're halfway to Golden, and we've lightened the load, what with the flour and bacon and other things we've eaten. I think there's room in the wagon for your extra dresses now. You don't have to wear all of them anymore."

Ma nodded. She didn't smile, but when she turned to me I saw her eyes flash as if she'd won some contest. "Whatever you think best, Thomas," she said.

As soon as Pa went off with Buttermilk John and three other men—they didn't invite Mr. Bonner to join them—I asked Ma, "Does Pa really mean it? May I wear just one dress now?"

Ma nodded, and then she smiled. "We kept our promise,

Emmy Blue. And we kept all of our clothes, too."

I started to take off my top dress, but Ma said it wasn't proper to undress right out there in the open. I'd have to wait until nooning. As we walked along beside the oxen, me holding the whip and tapping the lead ox every now and then, I wondered if Ma, in her good mood, would let me out of making all fourteen quilt squares. Maybe she would settle for eight or ten. But I knew she wouldn't.

Pa was right. The travel was easy that day. The air was cool, and the sun didn't beat down on us as it had for the last few days. In a mile or two, the mud turned hard, and the oxen moved more quickly. I wanted to find Joey and run off onto the prairie to search for birds' eggs or pick wildflowers, to dig my toes into the soft dirt and maybe lie down on my back in the prairie grass and look up at the clouds. Joey and I found wagons and animals and faces in the clouds, and we pointed them out to each other. Just the day before, he'd said, "That cloud looks like one of my pa's layer cakes!"

Today I knew I had to stay with the wagon. Pa had asked me to, and Ma was walking slower than usual. "You all right, Ma?" I asked.

"Of course, I am. What makes you ask?"

"I'm just asking," I said, but in truth I was worried about

her. We walked along in the damp earth, that made my feet and ankles and legs muddy. I hoped we'd come to a river before long and I'd be able to wash them. As the sun was reaching the top of the sky, I heard a shout and saw Pa and the other men returning. I called a halt, tapping our lead ox on the head with the whip and yelling, "Whoa."

"No need to stop, girlie," Mr. Bonner yelled at me. "Let them as was careless catch up with us."

I looked at Ma to tell me whether I should start up again, but Buttermilk John came abreast of us. "Ye called it right, Miss Hatchett. Time for our nooning," he said. He held up his arm as a signal, and the wagons came to a stop, turning out so that the women could prepare dinner and the men could unhitch the animals to graze.

Pa came toward us, huddled on the horse he had borrowed, and I thought maybe he'd been hurt. Ma did, too, because she quickly climbed down from the wagon, with the skillet in her hand and a worried look on her face. "Thomas?" she said.

Pa grinned as he opened his coat. Sitting on the saddle, shivering, was the sorriest dog I'd ever seen. He was an ugly mutt the size of a lamb, and he quivered when he looked up at Pa, his tail as limp as my sunbonnet had been in the rain. His coat was matted with dirt and burs, and he was so thin that his ribs stuck out. Pa let go of him, but the dog shook and didn't want to jump down. Pa nudged him off the saddle, and the dog huddled on the ground, looking up at Pa as if begging him for something.

"What in the world?" Ma said.

"It's a dog."

"I can see that. Whose dog?"

Pa shrugged.

"What are you doing with him?"

"I found him under a bush when we were searching for the runaway animals. I couldn't just leave him there to starve. Emmy Blue, get him a pan of water and one of your ma's cold biscuits."

I poured water into our skillet, and the dog lapped it up. Pa told me to fill it again.

Ma said, "Oh, for heaven's sake, Thomas. How can I use a pan that some stray dog's been drinking out of? Who knows what kind of sickness he's carrying."

"He needs water and food," was all Pa said.

I'd taken two biscuits left over from breakfast out of our food box and tossed them one at a time to the dog. He ate each in a single gulp and looked for more.

"Maybe he belonged to an Indian," Ma said.

"I doubt it," Pa answered. "He wandered off from a wagon train is my guess. Look, you can see a bit of rope tied about his neck."

"Well, wherever he came from, we're not taking him in. You said yourself, Thomas, we have no room." Ma looked a little triumphant at that. It was the first time she'd pointed out to him that we didn't have room in the wagon for something of his. Ma was stubborn. Although Pa had finally allowed a place for our clothes in the wagon, Ma wasn't ready to ease up on him.

"I want him, Ma," I suddenly said. "I had to give away Skiddles, and Pa wouldn't let me take the turtle we saw along the road. May I keep him?"

"He was somebody's pet, Meggie," Pa told her. "He'll make a good companion for Emmy Blue."

Ma put her hands to the small of her back and stretched. "Oh, I don't know. He's just another mouth to feed." Ma straightened up and twisted her hands in her apron.

"I'll take care of him," I pleaded.

The dog went up to Ma and whined, then sat down on top of her bare feet and looked up at her. While Ma stared at him, Aunt Catherine came up next to her. She had walked up from the back of the wagon train.

"He likes you, Meggie," Aunt Catherine said. "Whose dog is he?"

"He wants to be Emmy Blue's. Thomas found him when he was out looking for the runaway animals this morning. But I think he's just one more creature I'll have to care for."

"Emmy Blue will do it. Just look at how much she's helped on this trip. She's a responsible girl," Aunt Catherine said.

Ma studied me a moment. "She is that."

"Does that mean I can keep him?" I asked. The dog came up to me and thumped his tail. Maybe he knew I was defending him.

"He'd be good protection for Emmy Blue," Uncle Will spoke up. I hadn't seen him standing behind Aunt Catherine.

"Not much of one," Ma said. "He's just a bare-bones creature. I doubt he could walk all the way to Golden."

"I'll carry him," I said.

Ma looked around at all of us staring at her, then sighed. "It's four against one. Emmy Blue. I suppose you've got yourself a dog."

I grinned at Ma, then squatted down beside the dog and hugged him, feeling his bones through his coat. He needed a good scrubbing and his coat well combed, but I'd clean him up the next time we crossed a river. I'd wash him with the soap Ma had made from ashes before we'd left Quincy, and I'd use Pa's currycomb.

"What will you name him?" Pa asked.

"How about Wanderer," Aunt Catherine suggested.

"Or Brownie, because of the color of his coat," Uncle Will said.

Pa suggested Lucky.

But I had already heard Ma call the dog by his name. "I'm going to call him Barebones," I said.

- - - - - - - - -

After I fed Barebones some of my buckwheat cakes for lunch, he was my dog, and he followed me everywhere. I brushed his coat to get out the sticks and prickers, then used soap and water to wash him in our basin. He'd get a proper bath later. Except for being dirty and hungry, Barebones seemed to be healthy.

"Got you a mongrel, did you?" Mr. Bonner asked.

"Yes, sir."

"Most likely an Indian dog. You be careful. He's likely to go after you in the night. Might be crazy, too. Watch that he don't foam at the mouth. He bites one of my oxen, I'll put him down."

"Yes, sir." Ma had told me to be polite to Mr. Bonner and not to talk back to him. We didn't want to rile him for fear he'd turn on us—or Mrs. Bonner. But he made me angry, because I knew Barebones wasn't a wild dog. He'd been somebody's pet, because when I told him to stay or to sit, he minded me. And he knew how to play fetch. When I threw a stick, he brought it back. Barebones learned his name right off, and came whenever I called him, although I didn't have to do that very often because he stuck by my side.

"I believe Will was right. He will be good protection for Emmy Blue," Ma admitted after a few days.

"Ugly as he is, nobody will want to mess with him," Pa said, as he winked at me. We both knew that Ma had grown as fond of Barebones as we had. She fixed extra biscuits and pancakes every day to feed him, and after Pa shot an antelope, she put aside the bones for my dog.

Barebones followed me when I wandered away from the wagon train to search for buffalo chips. There were few trees on the prairie, so we couldn't use wood for our campfire. Sometimes we'd find a stick or a broken branch that we picked up along the trail, but now we had to burn buffalo chips, the huge circles of buffalo dung that dotted the prairie. They made a good fire and burned white hot. At first, Ma had refused to use them, but she'd learned that she didn't have any choice. It was either buffalo chips or no fire at all. Pa already knew that, so before we left Quincy, he'd packed a huge grain sack for collecting them.

It was my job to gather the chips. Joey collected them for his family, too. Each morning, we took our sacks and searched the prairie for the dung. The chips were good fuel, but they burned quickly, so we needed to gather all we could find. We looked for dried chips, because they burned better and were lighter weight. Barebones came with us. He thought we were playing and picked up sticks for me to throw to him.

"Let me toss one," Joey said.

"Sure." I threw the stick to him, and Joey flung it as far as he could, but Barebones brought it back to me. He knew he was my dog.

"I wish I had a dog," Joey said. "I had one at home, but Mama wouldn't let me take him. I bet when we get to Denver,

Papa will find a dog for me."

"You can come and visit us, and I'll let you play with Barebones."

"I'd like that."

We'd hunted for buffalo chips all morning. The sacks were heavy and our hands were dirty with the powdery dust. "We have enough," I told Joey. Then I spotted a chip that was so dry it was white. "One more," I said, dragging my sack to where the chip lay on a pile of rocks. I tossed a rock at the dung circle to see the white dust rise. Just as I did, I heard a noise like pebbles rattling in a tin cup. When I looked to see what it was, I spotted a rattlesnake coiled in the rocks, its tail shaking and making a warning sound. The snake raised its head, and its long red tongue flickered back and forth. I looked into its black eyes and froze in place with my arm out toward the buffalo chip.

I knew I should jump back, but I was held by the snake's stare. I tried to call Joey, tried to tell him to throw a stone at the snake or shake a stick at it to divert its attention. But my voice wouldn't work.

The snake, its tail shaking furiously, kept its gaze on me as its awful head moved slowly toward my arm. It was as if it knew I couldn't get away and was playing with me. Then just as it got close enough to strike, I saw a dark shape fly past me and grip the neck of the snake in its teeth. Barebones shook the snake back and forth, back and forth, the rattler flapping and twisting, until at last it was still, and Barebones dropped it into the dirt.

Joey ran over to me. "Barebones saved your life," he said. He found a stick and poked the rattler, but it didn't move.

I looked at my arm, still stretched out, and slowly lowered it. Then I hugged Barebones for all I was worth. "You saved my life, you ugly thing," I said, while Barebones licked my face.

Joey squatted beside the snake. "Pa says you can eat these things. They taste like chicken. You want it?"

"Not me." I shivered at the idea.

Joey took out a knife, and holding up the end of the snake, he cut off the rattles and handed them to me. "You'd better keep those, in case nobody believes what happened."

"Who wouldn't believe me?" I asked. Ma had taught me to tell the truth, so when I said something had happened, Ma and Pa knew it had.

Joey considered that. "Maybe Mr. Bonner."

I left that last buffalo chip where it was, just in case snakes came in pairs, and Joey and I dragged our sacks back to the wagons.

Before I could tell Ma and Pa what had happened, Joey burst out, "Emmy Blue almost got bit by a rattlesnake, the biggest one you ever saw. Show them the rattles."

I still had them in my hand, and opened it. Pa picked them up. Uncle Will came up to us then and eyed the rattles, saying, "Look at how many there are. That must have been a very large, very old snake!"

"What happened?" Ma asked. Her face was white, and her hands looked like they were shaking.

She looked so worried that I couldn't tell her, but Joey spoke up. "The snake was all coiled up and ready to bite her, but Barebones grabbed it in his teeth and shook it to death."

"If it wasn't for Barebones, I'd have been bit," I whispered.

"Hurrah for Barebones!" Joey said.

Ma put one hand on my arm and squeezed. With the other, she gripped the dog's fur. "You have a stout heart, Barebones," she said.

At the end of the week, when Ma asked what I would put into the drawer in the medicine chest where I kept my treasures, I handed her the rattles. "I want to save these," I said, "but these are the only ones I ever hope to get. One rattlesnake out on the prairie is enough for me."

Chapter Fourteen

POOR JOEY

*L*ucy Bonner wasn't the only woman on the wagon train who became our friend. Celia Potts was several wagons behind us, although she and her family often camped next to us. She was a tiny woman with curly red hair, freckles, and eyes the color of a robin's egg I'd once found. Ma called her looks unusual, and I thought that she might have been the prettiest woman I'd ever seen.

"She blazes like fire," Aunt Catherine said, and it was true. With her red hair, the colorful dresses she wore, and the way she always seemed to be in motion, Celia Potts did indeed resemble a blaze. She stood out among the drab women in the train.

Of course, there were reasons she was active. There were

her three children—Honor, a girl who was three, and Honor's two brothers, Bert, two, and Ulysses, who was born just before the Potts family started west. We had met Celia when she dashed between Uncle Will's wagon and ours, Ulysses in her arms, chasing Honor and her brother.

"I'll hold your baby, Mrs. Potts," I said now, as she tried to grab Honor and Bert with her free hand. I loved babies, and it was clear to me that there'd never be any more in our family. Agnes Ruth had died more than five years earlier, and Ma hadn't had any babies since then.

"I'd be obliged," she said, giving him up and grasping the other two children, one in each hand. "You are to call me Celia. I must be closer to you in age than to your mother. I'm nineteen," she said, glancing at Ma. She was right. I was almost eleven, while Ma was more than thirty.

I rocked Ulysses in my arms, and he smiled at me and made bubbly sounds. I loved that baby right off. We all adored Celia, too. We cared about her every bit as much as we did Lucy Bonner. Only there was a difference between them. While we disliked Mr. Bonner—Ma wouldn't let me use the word *hate* or I'd say I hated him—we loved Mr. Potts.

James Potts, unlike his wife, was big and dark with black hair to his shoulders and eyes the color of soot. And he had a voice that boomed out. I was a little afraid of him at first, but then I realized he was a kind man who loved his children. In the evenings, when most of the men sat and smoked their pipes after they'd finished working with the animals or repairing the wagons, Mr. Potts played with Honor and Bert, and he'd hold Ulysses so that Celia could visit with Ma, Aunt Catherine, and Mrs. Bonner.

Mr. Bonner heard Mr. Potts baby-talk to Ulysses, and he asked in a loud voice, "What kind of man talks with a child like that?"

"Why a man who loves his son," Mrs. Bonner told him. She didn't often talk back to Mr. Bonner, and I wondered if he'd be angry with her. We were used to seeing the bruises on her arms and face by then. She would always tell us she was careless, that she bumped into things, but I was sure that wasn't true. Sometimes we'd hear her crying in the night, and Mr. Bonner would shout, "Be still!" Ma would push back the blankets, but Pa would tell her to stay where she was.

Mr. Potts wasn't like that. When he grabbed his wife, it was to hug her. "Ain't she the prettiest thing?" he'd ask us. "Why would such a beauty marry an ugly cuss like me?"

"Because I couldn't do any better," she'd reply. "Besides, who else would take you?" Then they'd laugh as if she'd said the cleverest thing they'd ever heard. We'd laugh, too, just because they made us happy.

Ma hadn't known Celia for more than five minutes before she asked her usual question: "Do you quilt?"

"Oh no. With three little ones, I don't have time. It's all I can do to keep up with mending." She held out her freckled hands. "Besides, these fingers get too confused. They can't abide a thimble, either, so they're always getting pricked." She laughed. "You know that old saying that a woman has to complete thirteen quilt tops before she can get married? Well, I never finished but two, and a poor job I did of them. My friends expected me to be an old maid."

Aunt Catherine looked down at the quilt square that was rumpled up in my hand. We had been on our morning quilt walk when we stopped to visit with Mrs. Potts. "Did you know that, Emmy Blue? At the rate you're going, you'll not marry till you're fifty!"

"Or maybe never," I said, and the women laughed.

"Do you embroider, then?" Mrs. Bonner asked Celia.

"I tried that, too, but I dropped the stitches, so I laid it down."

"I could teach you to quilt," Ma told her. "If you don't want to learn now, then come along when you do."

"It would be a waste of time. I expect I am hopeless." Celia's mouth turned down in a pout. But just as quickly she smiled again. "I can paint. I decorated all my china with roses. Let me show you."

As Celia handed Ulysses to me and climbed into her wagon, Ma whispered, "Paint?" to Aunt Catherine, who shrugged.

Celia backed out of the wagon and jumped to the ground, holding a plate in her hand. The plate was covered with flour because, like our cups, her plates had been stored in her flour barrel. She wiped it on her apron and held it out. Painted on the plate was the most beautiful rose I'd ever seen, so real that I thought the thorn in the stem would prick me if I touched it.

Ma took the plate, holding it as if she was afraid it would break. "Why, I never saw anything so lovely. You are a real artist, Celia. Look, Catherine, there are even tiny dewdrops. If I held it in the sun, would they dry up?"

Aunt Catherine took the plate and examined it. Then she turned it over. "You ought to sign your name on the back. I've seen that on fine china."

Celia looked embarrassed. "I just paint. But I'm glad you like it. I brought my paints with me. Jimmy insisted. He said if he didn't find a gold mine, I could support us by painting china. I wouldn't mind that, but I doubt we could live on five cents a day. It's a good thing I don't have to earn my living." She laughed and took back the plate, balancing it carelessly in her hand.

I was holding Ulysses, and as Celia reached for him, he flung out his little arm, knocking the plate from her hand. It bounced on a rock, breaking in half, then landed on the dirt, broken into pieces."

"Oh my goodness!" Ma said, horrified. There were too many pieces to glue back together—if anyone in the wagon train even had glue. She reached down for the largest piece, which had a rose leaf painted on it. "This one is worth saving." She brushed off the dirt that was mixed with a little flour and held it out to Celia.

I thought Celia would be heartbroken, but she only laughed. "Keep it if you want it. Now I have an excuse to paint another. It's what I like to do best."

After she left, Ma told Aunt Catherine, "I'd have been heartbroken if I'd smashed that plate, but nothing seems to bother her. She might be the happiest woman I've ever met."

"She is that, and talented. Why, I'd hire her to paint a set of china—if I had any china," Aunt Catherine said.

"Maybe she'll paint tin plates," I told her.

After my scare with the rattlesnake, Joey and I were careful when we gathered buffalo chips. We weren't concerned when the chips were in the dirt, but we knew that snakes like to sun themselves on rocks. So we poked around with sticks before picking up the dung we found in rocky places. It was a good thing, because we saw other rattlers. Barebones barked at them to warn us, but he never attacked the snakes.

"How did he know that first snake was going to bite me?" I asked Pa.

He shrugged. "Sometimes animals are smarter than we are."

"I don't think one of the oxen would protect me," I said.

"I never said an ox was smart," Pa said, and laughed.

Joey and I were careful even when we weren't picking up buffalo chips. When we hunted for stones or birds' eggs or when we lay on the ground to look up at the sky, I kept a watch for snakes.

Joey teased me about it. "I'll bet the snakes send out smoke signals telling each other to keep away from Barebones," he said. Buttermilk John had told us that Indians communicated by waving blankets over their fires, directing the smoke a certain way.

Barebones might have protected me, but not Joey. One morning, Joey jumped out of the wagon and landed directly on a rattler. Before he even knew he'd stepped on the snake, the rattler sank its fangs into Joey's leg.

He screamed, screamed so loud that everybody in the camp heard him. The men dropped what they were doing and ran toward the Schmidt wagon. Mr. Potts grabbed an axe attached to the side of his wagon and rushed to my friend. When he reached the snake, Mr. Potts swung at it with the axe, chopping off its head. Ma and Pa and I reached Joey just as Mr. Potts cut the snake in half. Pa picked up Joey, holding him in his arms.

Buttermilk John was right behind us. "Lay him on the ground," he ordered.

Ma found a quilt from the wagon seat and spread it on

the ground for Joey.

The Schmidts, who had been gathering their oxen, didn't know Joey was the cause of the ruckus. When they reached their wagon and saw him, Mrs. Schmidt let out a scream louder than her son's.

Mr. Schmidt grabbed her arm and said that Buttermilk John was taking care of Joey. We all watched as Buttermilk John straightened the snake-bit leg. Then he took a sharp knife from his belt.

"Don't cut off his leg," Mrs. Schmidt yelled, pulling away from Mr. Schmidt.

Buttermilk John handed the knife to Pa and said, "Cleanse it in the fire."

Pa went to the Schmidts' fire and swiped the blade through the flame, then brought it back to where Buttermilk John knelt beside Joey. He had already taken a leather strap and tied it tightly around Joey's leg, above the spot where the snake had bitten him. He made two slashes above the bite. Then he put his mouth to the cuts and began to suck out blood and spit it onto the ground.

"What's he doing?" Mrs. Schmidt asked. She looked terrified and had begun to cry.

"He's sucking out the snake's venom that's in Joey's blood," Pa explained. "He's getting rid of all the poison."

"He won't lose the leg, will he, my Joey?" Mrs. Schmidt asked. There were tears running down her face. Mr. Schmidt steadied his hand on his wife's arm, but she flung it off.

"You, Schmidt!" she yelled. "This is your fault. You sacrificed your son so that we can go to that godforsaken place, that Denver. If we'd stayed at home where we belonged, Joey wouldn't have got bit by the snake."

Mrs. Bonner walked over to her and touched Mrs. Schmidt's face. "My dear, we are praying for Joey. Will you join us?" Ma and Aunt Catherine and some of the other women were standing at the back of the Schmidt wagon, their heads bowed.

Mrs. Schmidt seemed startled by the kindness. "I don't know. You ladies are praying for Joey?"

"Please," Mrs. Bonner said, leading Mrs. Schmidt to where the women stood.

Mrs. Schmidt didn't pray. She only stood there and muttered, "That Denver. Why did I ever like strawberry tarts?"

After a while, Buttermilk John said he had sucked out enough blood. He removed the strap from Joey's leg and stood up. "There're other things I could do, make a brine of salt and plantain, but I don't suppose anybody's got plantain." He looked down at Joey, then said, "We'll put him in the wagon. He'll ride there."

"We go on?" Mr. Schmidt asked.

Buttermilk John nodded. "We got to keep moving. The boy'll be out of his mind for a time. It's a natural thing. Don't let it cause ye to worry. It was a small snake and they can be meaner than the big ones. Still, this child thinks your boy will make it."

Some of the men began to move the furniture in the Schmidt wagon to make room for Joey. Ma motioned me to slip away from the women, and together we found blankets and quilts to make a pallet for my friend. Then the men lifted him into the wagon.

Pa and Uncle Will yoked the Schmidt oxen and chained them together, then attached the chains to the wagon. Mr. Schmidt went to his wife and took her arm. "Mama, Joey's in the wagon. We have to move on. Buttermilk John says so."

Mr. Schmidt helped his wife into the wagon, where she climbed in beside Joey. When she was settled, she put her head in her hands and began to cry again. I could hear her all the way back to our wagon.

I walked along beside our oxen, next to Pa. We were silent for a time. Then, trying to keep my voice steady, I asked, "Is Joey going to die, Pa?" I hadn't wanted to ask, because Pa always told the truth. I didn't want to give up hope.

Pa flicked the whip against his hand a time or two before he turned to me. "I don't know the answer, Emmy Blue. Nobody does. Buttermilk John says it depends on whether the snake was angry and injected a large quantity of venom into the bite. The bite would be worse if the snake was hungry, too. It also depends on how Joey's body fights the poison.

Right now, he's very sick, and when he wakes up, he'll be in pain. It'll be two or three days before we know whether he'll be all right. And if he is, it could be weeks before the pain and swelling go away."

"But he might be all right," I said, snatching at Pa's words. Ma always told me to hope for the best and that was what I was doing now.

Chapter Fifteen

GO-BACKS

---

*T*he camp was quiet that night, with no singing, no shouting. No one even yelled at the oxen. The children, too, seemed to be quieter than usual.

Joey wouldn't have cared about noise, because he hadn't awakened. When we stopped for the day, I went to the Schmidt wagon and asked if I could sit with him. Mrs. Schmidt had stopped crying and was sitting beside her son, stone-faced. She didn't say a word but handed me a bowl of water and a square of cloth she had used to wipe Joey's brow. Then she climbed out of the wagon.

"Hi, Joey. It's me, Emmy Blue—and Barebones," I said. My dog had climbed into the wagon and lain down near Joey.

Joey moaned and muttered words that I didn't understand.

For a time he thrashed around, but I held him with my hands, and he was still. I dipped the cloth in water and washed his face, because he was sweating. Barebones licked Joey's face, too. Joey was hot and had a fever. Once he called out, "Papa!" and another time, "Pretzel," which he'd told me was the name of the mutt he'd left behind.

I sat there for a long time until Mr. Schmidt relieved me, saying, "Thank you, little girl. You are Joey's friend. When we're in Denver, I'll bake a cake for you."

"For me—and Joey," I said, and Mr. Schmidt patted my head.

As soon as I got out of the wagon, I saw Ma standing with Mrs. Schmidt. I'd forgotten all about doing chores, and I thought she would be annoyed with me. Instead, she said, "You gave comfort, Emmy Blue."

Ma held a tin plate of biscuits. I noticed other women with food in their hands. At home, when a neighbor was hurt or sick, the women baked cakes and pies. They brought them, along with stews and vegetables and fruit from their orchards, to the family in need. That was what they were doing now. They couldn't bake or make custards or jellies, but they shared what they had. Even Mrs. Bonner came with a plate of food, and I wondered if it was her own supper. I doubted that her husband would have shared his food with anyone.

Mrs. Schmidt didn't seem to notice the women, but Mr.

Schmidt shook the hands of each woman and thanked her.

"How is Joey?" Ma asked me.

I shrugged. I'd never been around a snake-bit person before. "He was acting crazy. He cried and carried on, but he didn't wake up."

"That's called delirium," Ma explained.

"Oh, Ma, is he going to be all right?" I put my head against her and started to cry. I'd held back the tears all day, trying to be brave, not wanting to sound like Mrs. Schmidt, but now I couldn't help myself.

Ma put her arms around me. "He's still fighting. That's a good sign."

"If something happened to him, I don't know what I'd do. He's the only friend besides Barebones I've made on this whole trip."

"We will hope for the best. And pray. Buttermilk John is as good a doctor as we could have on the trail."

"If only—"

"Hush, we cannot change what has happened." She put her arm around me.

We watched while Pa and Mr. Potts lifted Joey out of the wagon and laid him on the ground. "He'll be cooler there," Ma explained. "They want to keep the fever down. Let's get fresh water and help sponge him off."

We went to our wagon where Ma dipped water into a washbasin, which I carried back to Mr. Schmidt. He was sitting beside Joey, and he smiled when I began to wipe Joey's face.

"He's better, don't you think so, Emmy Blue?" he asked.

I didn't want to hurt Mr. Schmidt, so I thought it was all right to tell a lie. "Much better." But I couldn't see any difference.

After a while, Pa told me it was time to go to our wagon. The women would take turns looking after Joey during the night. I should sleep so that I could sit with him again the next day, Pa told me. He would be better then.

But when daylight came, the only difference I could see was that Mrs. Schmidt had stopped crying, although she still blamed Mr. Schmidt for Joey's condition. She sat on the wagon seat while I crouched inside the wagon beside Joey, and she muttered at Mr. Schmidt, who was walking beside the oxen.

Inside, Joey murmured in his sleep, gibberish mostly, although once I thought he said, "Emmy Blue." I sang to him in a low voice, the way I sang to Ulysses Potts, and that seemed to calm him a little.

Joey was delirious for two days. The third morning, I was lifting his head to get him to drink a little water, when he opened his eyes and said, "My leg. It burns like fire."

I realized that he had come out of his delirium. "Mrs.

Schmidt!" I called. "Come quick!"

Both of the Schmidts heard me. Mr. Schmidt tapped the lead ox on the head and called, "Whoa." Then they climbed into the wagon.

"He's awake!" I cried. "He talked to me!" I was as happy as if it was my birthday.

The Schmidts pushed past me, and I climbed down the wheel and hurried to our wagon, shouting, "Ma! Ma!" I ran so fast I had to catch my breath before I could say, "Joey talked. He's going to be all right."

"Oh, Emmy Blue, thank God." Ma took a deep breath while I looked toward the wagon behind us. Mr. Bonner was scowling, as he always did, but Mrs. Bonner and Celia, who was walking beside her, clasped their hands together and lowered their heads. I knew they were thanking God for making Joey better.

That night, a Saturday, there was singing, and Buttermilk John danced a jig with Celia. Buttermilk John told us it would be several days before Joey could walk, and then he'd have to use a stick because he couldn't put pressure on the leg. It might be weeks before he would be back to normal. He was still a sick boy, but he was going to be okay. We were all relieved, and Mr. Potts found a straight branch, stripped it of bark, and carved it, which he presented to Joey as a walking stick.

"I feel as if we've all come out of a dark place together,"

Ma said.

We were happy that Joey was better, although Mrs. Schmidt didn't stop complaining. We heard her continue to yell at her husband, blaming him because Joey had almost died. I heard Joey plead, "Mama, I'm okay."

"You are okay? How do you know? This is what happens to us when we leave our home."

The guards didn't need to pound on a dishpan to wake the camp that morning, as they usually did, because Mrs. Schmidt had already awakened us. She cursed her husband and then she began to throw his baking pans and mixing spoons out of the wagon."

"No, Mother," Mr. Schmidt begged.

"We must go back," she yelled.

"Please, Ma," Joey pleaded. "I want to go to Denver with Pa."

"No. I do not go a step farther. Go ahead if you want to, but I am not going with you!"

Mr. Schmidt stepped out of their wagon and walked past ours to where Buttermilk John was helping someone yoke a stubborn ox. "I talk to you," Mr. Schmidt said. His shoulders were slumped, and he didn't look Buttermilk John in the eye.

Buttermilk John seemed to understand what was going on. "Going back, are ye?"

Mr. Schmidt nodded. "I don't have the choice. You heard her. We got to go on back. She says bad luck comes in twos.

If we go on, who knows what happens."

"Could be bad luck going back, too. Alone like that, ye'll be easy prey for Indians or anybody that ain't up to good. What if ye break your leg or the oxen take sick? Ye'd be on your own."

"I tell her that, but she won't listen." Mr. Schmidt looked at the ground, and I could see the sadness on his face. "I never wanted to get rich. I thought Colorado would be a nice place for Joey to grow up. She doesn't understand."

He started back toward his wagon, and when he passed us, Pa said, "Schmidt, good luck."

"Ya, you, too, Hatchett," Mr. Schmidt replied.

"I'll help you hitch your oxen," Pa said.

I followed behind and stopped at the wagon when I saw Joey peering out the back. "Your pa says you're leaving," I told him.

"If I hadn't stepped on that snake, we wouldn't have to." There were tears on his cheeks. I didn't know if they were there because he was in pain or if he was disappointed about turning back. "Darn snake!" he said.

"I'll miss you," I said, feeling shy.

"Me, too." He turned and reached into a pocket in the wagon cover. "I got something for you." He held out his hand. Inside was a rock that was the color of a pigeon's egg. When we'd spotted it, we thought it was a snake's egg. I'd wanted it, but Joey'd seen it first, so it was his.

"That's your egg-rock," I said. "It's your favorite thing."

"Take it for good luck," Joey said. "Besides, I want some-thing of mine to get to Denver. I want you to remember me, to remember me as something besides a go-back."

I took the rock, feeling sorry I didn't have anything to give him in return. But as I put the treasure into my pocket, I felt something and pulled out the quilt square I had finished the day before Joey was bitten. I hadn't worked on my piecing since then and had forgotten it was in my pocket. It was wadded up, and I ironed it between my hands. "Here." I held it out.

"Your quilt square? How can you make a quilt without it?"

I shrugged. "I don't care. I want you to remember me, too."

Ma came up to the wagon then, and I got down. Then we stood back as the Schmidts turned their team around and started east.

"How come Mrs. Schmidt acted the way she did?" I asked Ma. "You didn't want to go west either, but you never complained like that."

Ma patted my arm. "I believe we have to look on the good side of things."

Buttermilk John told us it was time to line up, and the men pulled their wagons into place. But I stood where I was, watching the Schmidt wagon get smaller and smaller. Joey waved from the back, framed in the puckered oval made by the wagon cover. Every now and then, Mr. Schmidt raised his whip hand in a farewell gesture. Mrs. Schmidt never turned around, I noticed. I watched them until I couldn't see them anymore. Then I turned and hurried to catch up with our wagon.

"Does bad luck really come in twos?" I asked Pa as the two of us walked beside the oxen. "That's what Mrs. Schmidt thinks. Maybe the Indians will get them."

"I doubt there's an Indian on the prairie who'd want to get between Mrs. Schmidt and her tongue," Pa said with a chuckle. Then he said. "Maybe if she complained less, her luck would improve. Luck is what you make it."

I pondered that as we walked, and decided that Pa might be right. But later I wondered if maybe the wagon train, not the Schmidts, had bad luck.

Mr. Potts had always been careful with his rifle, putting it out of reach of Honor and Bert. As young as they were, the two of them knew they'd be punished if they touched it. Mr. Potts carried the gun carefully, pointing it at the ground, aiming the barrel away when he set it down. He kept it loaded all the time. If a snake or a mad dog was about to strike or if Indians attacked, a rifle wasn't much good if it wasn't loaded.

So the accident didn't make any sense. Mr. Potts might have been spooked by a dog or by the sudden movement of an ox. All we know was something caused the gun to go off. It wasn't unusual to hear a shot far off, but it was the middle of the day, and we had just stopped for the nooning. The shot had come from the camp. I thought somebody must have aimed at a snake, because after Joey was bitten, everybody was worried about rattlers.

We turned in the direction of the Potts's wagon but didn't see anything at first. Then we heard Celia scream and saw her husband fall to the ground. "Help! Jimmy's been shot!" she called.

Pa rushed to the Potts's wagon, with Ma and me close behind him. By the time we arrived, others were already there. They had stretched Mr. Potts out on the ground. Ma reached for my arm to stop me, but I brushed past her and stared down at Mr. Potts. His shirt was bloody, and I heard a man say, "Poor fool shot hisself in the belly."

"Is it bad?" someone asked.

"Gut-shot is as bad as it gets."

Ma reached for my arm again and tried to pull me away, but Pa stopped her. "Emmy Blue's old enough to see what a gun can do," he said.

I wasn't sure that was true, but I couldn't keep myself from looking. Ma held me tight as we watched Buttermilk John kneel down and try to stop the bleeding with a wadded up shirt. He shook his head and stood up. "Nothing this child can do. I'm sorry, missus."

Celia knelt beside her husband. "Jimmy. Oh, please wake up, Jimmy," she cried.

He moved his hand a little, and she grasped it. Then he turned his head to the side and I could see him take one deep breath. It was his last.

It happened so fast. I was too surprised to cry. One minute Mr. Potts was standing by his wagon, and the next he was gone.

"It's over," Ma said, kneeling beside Celia. And then Ma helped her to stand.

"But Jimmy ...," Celia said.

"The men will take care of him. We will plan a service."

Celia tried to pull away, but Ma held her. "You must tell me Jimmy's favorite hymns," she said gently. "And you must paint a marker for him, paint it with your roses on it."

I was in a daze, but I knew I had to do something. I went to the Potts's wagon to get the children. Aunt Catherine and I took Ulysses, along with Honor and Bert, to our wagon to play. Pa and Uncle Will and some of the other men went to find shovels to dig a grave. Buttermilk John said we'd stop for the rest of the day, and everyone agreed, even Mr. Bonner.

Late in the afternoon, we laid Mr. Potts to rest. He was put in the grave wrapped just in a quilt, because there was no extra wood to make a coffin. We sang "A Mighty Fortress is

Our God" and "O God, Our Help in Ages Past," while one man played the pump organ and another a fiddle. Then Uncle Will read from the Bible. Mrs. Bonner gave a prayer. Ma tried to lead Celia away as the men covered up her husband's body with dirt, but she insisted on staying. When the men were finished, they collected rocks and laid them on top of the grave to keep the wolves from digging it up. Then Celia placed a marker on the grave between two large rocks. She had made the marker from her breadboard and decorated it with roses. Across the top she'd painted, "James Potts, 1837-1864, Beloved Husband and Father. Good-bye, Jimmy. We'll meet in heaven."

While I held Ulysses, Celia took the hands of her two other children and stared at the grave, until Ma put an arm around her. Ma told her that Pa would collect her oxen in the morning when he gathered ours. "Emmy Blue will come with you to help with the children. She knows how to drive oxen, too," Ma said.

Pa did indeed bring in the Potts's oxen the following morning. He left them with Celia and returned to our campfire for breakfast. Then the two of us went to the Potts's wagon to make sure everything was in order to move out. I was proud that Ma and Pa thought I could drive the oxen by myself.

When we got there, Paul and Charlie Pitkin, two bachelor brothers who were going to Colorado Territory to farm, were helping Celia and the children into the wagon. The Pitkins were steady men, always willing to do their share of work, Pa said. He'd told me once that the Pitkins weren't a lot of fun, but you'd sure want them with you in time of trouble.

"Your girl's a mite young to be in charge of the oxen," Charlie Pitkin told Pa. "Being as there's two of us, we thought we could help Mrs. Potts drive her team."

His brother nodded. "Least we can do to help a neighbor."

I looked up at Celia, who was sitting on the wagon seat, holding Ulysses. She sat very still, as if she were a jumping jack that had been broken and couldn't fling its arms and legs around anymore. "I'll come tend Ulysses later," I told her.

She barely moved her lips to say, "Thank you."

Ma looked surprised when Pa and I returned. "Emmy Blue isn't driving the oxen?" she asked.

"The Pitkin boys," Pa told her.

Ma nodded. "They are good men."

Chapter Sixteen

INDIANS!

I missed Joey. I had plenty to do, tending Celia's three
children when she needed me. I helped Ma even more with
the cooking and laundry, because the journey had sapped her
strength. She rode in the wagon much of the time now.

The other children in the train were either younger or
older than I was, so there was nobody for me to play with.
There was Waxy to keep me company, but she had to stay in
the wagon, because the hot sun would melt her, and after
Joey, she wasn't as much of a companion as she had been
before I met him. There was Barebones, of course, but except
for him, I was by myself much of the time. I wandered out
onto the plains, but it wasn't any fun lying on the ground
with just my dog and finding images in the clouds. I couldn't

point them out to *him*. And gathering buffalo chips had become just one more chore. Even Barebones let me down after a while. He liked to go with Pa when Pa hunted antelope. So I didn't always have him with me when I explored the prairie.

I still looked for rocks and feathers, dried leaves and snake skins, but there was nobody to share my treasures with. Sometimes I'd just find a place to sit down and think about Joey, about the trip west, and whether we, too, ought to have gone back home.

I didn't want to, of course. I decided Ma didn't either. She said she was beginning to like the prairie, even though it was nearing summertime now, and getting very hot. We had come a long way, and soon we'd see the tips of mountains. Every day I searched the horizon, but I hadn't spotted them yet. We'd crossed the Mississippi and the Missouri. We'd seen Indians and death. My friend had turned back, but I'd found a new one in Barebones. I'd grown up, too. Ma said that I'd been a little girl when we left Quincy but had become almost a young woman over the last months.

"Our girl is growing up. I'm proud of her," Pa said, then laughed. "I sure hope that after all this work we went to raise her, she doesn't get snatched up by an Indian."

I'd worried about Indians ever since Pa announced we were going west. The first thing Abigail had said after I told her we were moving to Golden was, "Be careful you don't get shot dead with an arrow."

We'd seen Indians in St. Joe, of course, but they were beggars, and not like the Indians who came near our camp on the prairie. We could always spot them riding far off or sitting on their ponies, watching the wagons pass. A few times they came closer, and wandered into our camp. Buttermilk John said they wouldn't hurt us. If they were warriors, he told us, they wouldn't have brought their wives and children with them. But he did say they might rob us. "Ye'd be wise to keep a sharp watch. But it wouldn't hurt to share your food with them," he told us.

One night an Indian family came to our campfire. The father pointed to his mouth and said, "Beeskit, ko-fee." Ma, who had just taken a pan of biscuits out of the skillet, held it out to him. The Indian man ate them all, making Ma frown.

The man pointed to his mouth and said, "More, more." Ma set the rest of the biscuits on the plate, but this time, she set the plate in front of the woman and children. "They can eat their fill before I give another bite to that greedy man," Ma said. I hoped the Indian man didn't understand English.

After the family had eaten, the woman took a pair of beaded moccasins from her dress pocket and held them out for Ma to see. Then the woman pointed to me.

"She wants to trade," Buttermilk John explained. He took the moccasins and studied them. "Fine work, this."

"Emmy Blue could use moccasins. I don't like her stepping

barefoot on rocks and thorns," Ma said. "What does she want for them?"

"I reckon a handful or two of flour."

"That's little enough," Ma said.

The woman held out a buckskin sack, and Ma filled it. Then as the woman touched her children to move them along, Ma said, "Wait." She went to the wagon and came back with a large scrap of the bright red fabric that Aunt Catherine had bought for her in St. Joseph. Putting one hand over her heart, she gestured to the Indian woman with the material. "For you."

The woman stared at Ma but didn't speak or even smile. She took the fabric, rubbing it between her fingers, then showed it to her children as she said something in her native language. The little girl touched the cloth, and then smiled at me.

"She likes it. That was nice, Ma." I said.

"I can't imagine there's a woman, white or red, who can resist pinching a bit of yard goods between her fingers," Ma said.

I went to sleep that night and dreamed about living on the plains like the family that came to our campfire, galloping on my own horse across the prairie.

- - - - - - - - -

The heat often made me tired, and when we'd pass shady areas, I would sometimes stop to rest with my quilt squares. I still didn't care much for quilting, but I liked it better now that I had the hang of it, and especially now that the squares were almost done. It surprised me how much I could sew just walking along. It would be nice if Waxy had a coverlet, I decided the next morning, since Honor Potts had borrowed the one Abigail had given me for her rag doll and I hadn't wanted to ask for it back.

Thinking about my Log Cabin quilt, I removed a square from my pocket, my last one. I had walked out in front of the wagons, so I had time to sit and work on the quilt square before the train passed by. Pa had warned me not to lose sight of the wagons, but ours was a long train and slow, so I had plenty of time. There was a ravine lined with rocks, and after checking for rattlesnakes, I sat down on one of the rocks in the sun and set the pieces next to me. There were four left to attach to that square, and I spread them out in order before I began stitching. If I hurried, I figured, I could get all four of them attached before the train moved beyond me.

The sun was hot, and my fingers perspired, making the needle damp. It squeaked as I pushed it through the fabric. I finished the first strip, then the second. As I worked on the third, the wagon train finished passing me. Finally, I started on the fourth strip, pinning it to the square and taking tiny, neat stitches, the way Ma had taught me. At last, I was finished!

All I had left to do was sew the squares together. Now I was truly happy I'd made the quilt.

I folded the square and placed it in my pocket, thinking I ought to find our wagon. But I decided to sit a bit longer. It was so hot. I tried fanning myself with my hand, but that didn't help, so I leaned back against the rocks and turned my head to the side, out of the sun, to rest for just a moment. Before I knew it, I had fallen asleep.

I didn't know how long I slept. When I awoke, the trail was dusty in both directions, and I tried to remember which way the wagons had been headed. I thought I heard chains clanking in the distance, but I wasn't sure. I knew we followed the sun, but the sky had clouded over while I slept. A coyote ran past in the sagebrush. I'd heard coyotes howling at night and had seen them slinking along behind the wagons, their yellow teeth like saw blades.

I started in the direction of the noise. Pa wouldn't like it that I'd dawdled. I couldn't have been asleep that long, maybe only a few minutes, I thought. But as fast as I ran, I couldn't seem to see where the wagons were. I stopped and listened, but I didn't hear anything now. What if I were going in the wrong direction? That worry gave me an idea, and I crouched down to see if I could make out animal prints. That would tell me the direction the wagon train had taken, I decided. But the wind had come up, and I couldn't make out the prints. I wandered off the trail a little, hoping to spot boot prints in the sand.

And then I heard something, a horse, and I looked up to see a rider coming toward me in the distance. Maybe Ma had missed me and had sent someone to find me! I stood on the trail and waved my arms, jumping up and down to attract the man's attention. Maybe it was Pa, and he'd borrowed a horse. Or it might have been Buttermilk John. But as the horse drew nearer, I saw it was an Indian man on the horse, and I froze in fear. When I could make my legs work, I began to run. Maybe he hadn't seen me, I thought, and I could hide in the rocks until he passed by. But before I had gone ten steps, the Indian was right beside me. He reached down and pulled me up in front of him onto his horse. He held me so tightly that I couldn't move, and the terrible stories I'd heard about Indians filled my mind. He would either kidnap or kill me, I was certain.

I jerked to one side, ready to jump off the horse, but the man held me tight.

"Let me go," I shouted. "Pa'll come looking for me, Pa and the other men. They have guns."

The man didn't even look at me, and I wondered if he understood English. He kicked his horse into a trot as I said, "Take me to the wagon, you."

He only grunted, and when I tried to kick him, he slapped my leg.

"I'll give this to you if you'll let me go," I said, digging the quilt square out of my pocket and holding it up. Ma had said men didn't care about quilts, but I knew Indian men liked bits of fabric. I'd seen it woven into their braids or stitched to their shirts. Besides, it was the only thing I had to offer. But the Indian only glanced at it, as if he didn't want it any more than I had when I'd opened Grandma Mouse's present. I wished I had a knife or a ball of string to offer.

I struggled to get loose again, but the Indian held me with one arm. He pointed with his chin, saying, "Look."

I raised my head and could barely make out two men running toward us—Pa and Uncle Will, with Barebones barking beside them. I tried to wave, but my arms were pinned to my side. So I yelled as loud as I could, "Here I am, Pa!"

The Indian stopped the horse then and waited for Pa and Uncle Will to reach him. I wondered if he would try to sell me. But he set me down on the ground and watched as I ran toward Pa.

"He was going to steal me," I said as Pa put his arms around me and patted me on the back. I wanted to cry, but I wouldn't let the Indian man know how he had frightened me, so I held back my tears.

Pa shrugged. "If he was going to steal you, he wouldn't be riding toward the wagons."

The man seemed to understand Pa, and nodded his head once.

Pa went to the Indian and held out his hand, but the man didn't know what to do with it. Then the Indian held out his hand, palm up, and Pa said, "I believe he expects a little something for rescuing you, Emmy Blue."

Pa gestured toward the wagon train, and we all made our way toward it—Pa, Uncle Will, and me walking, and the Indian man riding his horse.

Ma saw us approach and stopped our wagon. When she saw the Indian man, she asked, "What is happening, Thomas?"

"This man found Emmy Blue, and it appears he was bringing her to us. I believe we owe him something."

Ma hugged me tight. "What do we have that he could possibly want? Surely he isn't interested in nails and a hammer."

"I'll give him my penknife, but he ought to have something more."

While Pa took out his knife and showed the Indian man how to open and close it, Ma took down her kettle with the bail handle and filled it with flour and pieces of sugar cone. She put her hand on the Indian's arm and smiled at him. "Thank you," she said, handing him the pot.

The man seemed pleased with the gifts. He nodded solemnly at Ma and Pa, and then he touched me on the head. I looked up, as the Indian held out his hand.

"What does he want?" I asked.

"You must give him something," Pa said, and I thrust out both my hands, palms up, and shrugged, to show him I didn't have anything for him. What if he wanted Waxy or Barebones? No! They were the only friends I had left.

The man reached down and put his hand into my apron pocket. Then he turned his horse around and galloped off.

"He took your quilt square," Ma said.

"I told him he could have it if he took me back to the wagons," I said. "But I didn't think he understood."

Pa shook his head. "What in the world will he do with it?"

Ma smiled. "Why, he'll do what any man would do. He'll give it to his wife."

We all laughed, but then I wailed, "Now with the block I gave to Joey and the one the Indian took, I'm two squares short. What if I've done all this work and can't finish the quilt?"

"This will help." Ma took her sewing basket out of the wagon and reached inside. Then she handed me a perfect Log Cabin square. "I made it for you after you gave the square to Joey. But there were only enough of the different colors to make one square. You'll have to do what quilters have always done when they run out. You'll make do." She reached into her scraps and removed the bright red piece from St. Joseph and cut it the same size as a finished Log Cabin square. You can use this."

"But Waxy's quilt will be spoiled. I made thirteen squares. You made one, and now I have to come up with another."

Ma only smiled. "You'll have an exciting story to tell your own little girl when she's ten years old."

Chapter Seventeen

HELLO, TOMMY

That night, Ma, Aunt Catherine, and I spread out my finished Log Cabin squares on top of our cutting board. Ma reminded me that the quilt squares themselves contained a pattern and the way the squares were arranged with their dark and light sides formed a second pattern. As she arranged them, she told me their names.

I moved the squares to form the different patterns she'd shown me, but each time I tried to use the red square in place of the missing block—in a corner or along the side—I had trouble. "I don't know where to put it," I said.

"Maybe you should hide it in plain sight," Aunt Catherine suggested.

That gave me an idea. I set the red square in the center

of the cutting board and spread the blocks around it. That was just the way the strips of each square went around the red center.

Aunt Catherine clapped her hands. "The red square is the heart of this quilt. You've come up with an entirely new design, Emmy Blue. What will you call it?"

I shook my head. "I'll have to think of something."

"How about Red Square in the Middle," Pa said, looking over our shoulders at the board.

"Too obvious," Aunt Catherine said. "Maybe Emmy Blue's Cabin."

I shook my head. That sounded silly.

"I know what to call it," Ma said.

"What?" I asked her.

"Indian Rescue."

I couldn't have thought of a more perfect name for my quilt.

Walking in the June sun made us more tired than usual, especially Ma. "This infernal heat!" she said when we stopped to rest. "Thank goodness we're not still wearing all those dresses. How many more miles before we reach Golden?"

"Not so many, I think," Aunt Catherine replied.

I was surprised that I missed having a quilt square in my

pocket to work on. I'd grown to like my quilt walks—not that I would tell Ma, because she might come up with another quilt for me to work on.

"Time to go on," Aunt Catherine said, and we plodded after the wagons. By the time we caught up with Pa and Uncle Will, the train was stopped for the evening. Aunt Catherine told Ma to sit in the shade of the wagon while she and I prepared supper.

I had learned to mix biscuit dough, and I took out the flour and leavening and butter. Each morning, Ma bought cream from a family traveling with a cow and put it into a bucket that she hung from our wagon, just like the woman we'd met at our first river crossing had done. The movement of the bucket as it swung back and forth all day churned the cream into butter, leaving a little pool of buttermilk. I added the buttermilk to the flour mixture, stirred it with a fork, and pinched off large bits of dough. I dropped the dough into the skillet and put on the lid. When I was finished, Aunt Catherine set the pan on the coals of the fire.

"Is Ma sick?" I asked as I got out bones for my dog.

Aunt Catherine picked up the kettle and poured hot water over tea leaves in Ma's cup. She put down the kettle and studied me for a moment. "Your ma is fine."

"You can tell me, Aunt Catherine. I'm not a little girl anymore."

"You sure aren't a little girl anymore. You've walked

hundreds of miles, and you've done your share of work. I'm telling you the truth. There's nothing wrong with your ma that a little time won't take care of. She's tired from walking. She's not used to it. Of course, none of us have ever done this much walking. But your ma ..." She stopped and checked the tea.

"My ma what?" I asked when Aunt Catherine didn't continue.

"Some women are just better made for walking, I guess. Don't worry about her."

Still, I did worry. "I told Pa once that she was doing poorly, but I don't think he noticed."

"Oh, he noticed." Aunt Catherine smiled a little.

I lifted the lid off the skillet to see if the biscuits were browning, and as I did, the wind picked up, blowing dirt over the big pan.

"They say you have to eat a peck of dirt before you stop being a tenderfoot," Aunt Catherine said, changing the subject. "Well, I expect I stopped being a tenderfoot by the time we crossed the Missouri." Aunt Catherine rose from the fire with Ma's cup of tea, and we said no more about Ma's health.

At supper, Ma was too tired to eat the biscuits or anything else. Aunt Catherine fussed over her, telling her she had to keep up her strength, but Ma said food made her sick. When she saw I'd overheard that, she said, "It's the heat, Emmy Blue. You know eating in hot weather gives me the stomachache."

I knew no such thing, but I figured they weren't going to tell me what was ailing Ma no matter what I said, so there was no point in my trying to find out.

Ma went to sleep after that, but I could tell she didn't sleep well. She muttered and tossed off the blanket. I awoke in the night and heard her moaning. Pa and Aunt Catherine and Uncle Will were crowded around her, and Mrs. Bonner knelt in the dirt at her side. I got up, too, but Pa said Ma had had a bad dream and they were trying to quiet her.

When I woke up the next time, I knew something was wrong. The sun was shining and we should have moved out at daylight. I sat up and saw that the other wagons were gone. Our wagon and Uncle Will's sat alone on the prairie.

"Why are we still here? Did the oxen run off?" I asked.

Pa was standing by the campfire, a cup of coffee in his hand. He looked tired.

"Did we reach Golden?" But even as I asked, I knew that couldn't be. There were no mountains. Besides, we hadn't gone anywhere during the night.

"Golden's nearly a hundred miles yet," Pa said. "We'll catch up with the other wagons before nightfall. We were just waiting for you to wake up. There's a surprise for you."

I looked around until I spotted Ma, who was lying under a quilt in the shade of the wagon. "I don't understand. Is Ma bad sick?"

"No, not sick at all. She's fine. Come and see what she has." Pa took my hand and led me to the wagon, while Aunt Catherine and Uncle Will smiled at me.

Ma's quilt lay spread over the rubber blanket, with another quilt on top of her. She moved the coverlet a little, and I saw the tip of a tiny head covered with black hair. At first, I thought Pa had found another dog, but in a second I knew I was wrong. "A baby?" I asked.

Ma nodded. She moved the quilt so that I could see the little face, eyes closed.

"Whose baby?" I asked.

"Why he's ours. He was born last night," Ma said.

"We have a baby?" I couldn't have been more surprised if Pa had said we were turning around and going back to Quincy. I'd given up hoping we'd ever have another baby. I stared at the tiny head, my eyes wide. I blinked back tears. Then I knelt down beside Ma and put my arms around her.

"This is your brother," Ma said. She held out the infant, who was wrapped in one of Pa's soft shirts. "Do you want to hold him?"

"Put your arm under his neck," Pa said, but I knew that already. I was good with babies. After all, I'd taken care of Ulysses.

"What's his name?" I asked.

"I favor Tommy, for your father," Ma told me.

"Hello, Tommy," I said, cradling him in my arms, smiling

at the red, wrinkled face. His wiry hair reminded me of a coconut I'd once seen in a store. "Hi, Coconut Head," I whispered.

"He ought to have waited until we reached Golden, but he wouldn't," Pa said with a smile.

"We didn't expect him so soon," Aunt Catherine added. "The baby things must be at the bottom of the wagon, under all the lumber. It would take us a day to unpack and find them. I guess the poor little fellow will just have to be wrapped up in a great big quilt until we can find the one your ma put aside for him."

The quilt Tommy was wrapped in looked too big for such a tiny baby. I could ask Honor Potts to return Waxy's quilt, I thought, but that quilt would be too small for a baby. And then I remembered something. I handed Tommy back to Ma. "I have an idea," I said. I climbed into the wagon.

It took me a while to find the quilts. By the time I did , Pa and Uncle Will had yoked the oxen and chained them to the wagon. Aunt Catherine had stored the dishes and pots and stamped out the fire. Now she was taking Tommy from Ma and helping Ma stand. "Here's a quilt for Tommy," I said, and handed them the bundle that was in my arms.

"Where in the world ...," Aunt Catherine said as Ma took the quilt and unfolded it.

"Oh, Emmy Blue, I couldn't," Ma said, holding up Agnes Ruth's Memorial quilt, the one she had made in remembrance of my little sister after she died. It was small, just the size for a baby. "I never meant to use this." She ran her hand over the embroidered words: "Agnes Ruth, God's Precious Child, 1859."

"And just why not?" Aunt Catherine asked. "What better way to remember Agnes than to use her quilt for your son. After all, Agnes is his sister every bit as much as Emmy Blue is. And Tommy is God's precious child, too. I think Agnes would be honored that her quilt was used to keep her brother safe and warm."

Ma thought about that for a long time, and then she smiled at me. "You are right, both of you. All of my children are precious to me. Emmy Blue, you have made Agnes a happy part of our family again."

Chapter Eighteen

CELIA MAKES A DECISION

*T*thought the days would never pass after that. Each time we came to a hill, I rushed to the top of it, hoping I'd be the first one to spot the mountains. I asked Pa if he couldn't make the oxen go faster, but he told me we'd reach Denver soon enough.

Sometimes, I carried Tommy as I walked along, and Barebones and I showed him off to women in other wagons. My quilt walk had turned into a baby walk.

"It's not easy having a baby on the prairie like this," one woman said.

"We should have stopped a day for your mother to rest, but the men wouldn't hear of it," another added. "They'd stop for an ox with sore feet, I imagine, but not for a woman out of childbed. It's a hardship for a woman to go west, especially with little ones. I'd be a go-back if I could."

As I handed Tommy to Ma, I asked if *she*'d be a go-back if she could. Tommy would be a good excuse.

Ma took Tommy and held him in Agnes's quilt, then tucked him into the box in which we'd once stored the cooking pots. Ma was afraid Tommy would get too much prairie sun, so most of the time he rode in the wagon. "No," she replied. "Now that I have two children, I want to raise them in the clear, clean Colorado air."

I remembered how Aunt Catherine had complained the first day of our journey, and asked her, "Do you like things better now too?"

"Lots better. Sometimes I feel almost as free as a man out here." Then she laughed, and added, "That is, until I have to cook supper or wash clothes."

I left them and wandered back to Celia's wagon and climbed up to sit on the bench with her. I liked playing with the Potts children and chatting with Celia, although she'd become quiet and serious since her husband died. I wondered if she'd ever be happy again. The children were too small to walk much, and Ulysses couldn't walk at all, so they spent most of their time in the wagon. Sometimes, when I was there to keep an eye on the three little ones, Celia got out of the wagon and walked along beside Charlie Pitkin, who drove her oxen now.

"What's she going to do when we reach Denver?" I asked Ma and Pa.

"Oh, she'll find something," Pa answered.

We saw Lucy Bonner walking toward us, and I whispered, "Maybe Celia could go back, and Mrs. Bonner could go back with her."

"That's none of our affair," Pa said. He didn't see Ma catch my eye and shake her head, which I knew meant I should keep my mouth shut.

Pa flicked his whip at the oxen, and Ma and I waited for Mrs. Bonner.

"I was hoping to hold Tommy," Mrs. Bonner said.

"I'll get him," I told her, and Pa stopped the oxen long enough for me to climb into the wagon for the baby.

As I got out, holding Tommy, I heard Mrs. Bonner say, "I wanted to stay with you the morning after Tommy was born. I told Owen it was the right thing to do. But he said my place was with him. And you know how anxious he is to reach Denver. So please forgive me for not being a better neighbor."

"You helped deliver Tommy," Ma said. "I could not have given birth to him without your help."

"Oh yes, I think you could have." Mrs. Bonner chuckled.

I handed the baby to Mrs. Bonner, who touched Tommy's tiny forehead with her fingers and sang him part of a lullaby. "I wish Owen liked children," she said, more to herself than to us. "He told me he'd as soon throw them to the dogs."

Ma and I stared at each other. I'd never heard such a horrible thing.

"And me with them. My husband does not believe I am a very good wife." Tears began to roll down Mrs. Bonner's cheeks, and she rubbed her eyes. "Oh, the dust is bad here. It makes me cry." But I knew that was not why she was crying.

When she had wiped away the tears, Mrs. Bonner raised her head and said, "He is right. A good wife would never complain about her husband, as I am doing. I am untrue to Owen in that way."

"And he is untrue to you in treating you in such a beastly manner," Ma told her.

Instead of being angry with Ma, Mrs. Bonner burst out, "Oh, Meggie, marriage is not what I thought. I should never have married without knowing him better. I have done a terrible thing, and now I shall spend my life regretting it."

Ma put her arm around Mrs. Bonner.

"I should not burden you with this," Mrs. Bonner continued, "but you, Catherine, and Celia are my only friends now that I have left home. I don't know how I shall go on. Once we reach the mountain camps, when there is no one around to come to my aid, I fear for my safety."

"He has already shown he is not a good man," Ma said. "You must rid yourself of him."

"You mean leave him?" Mrs. Bonner looked confused. "How can I do that? We are married. I would be disgraced.

My family would never take me back."

"Would you rather they take you back in a wooden box?" Ma asked firmly. "If your husband continues to beat you as he does, he may inflict serious harm. Forgive me for speaking frankly, Lucy. Thomas says it is not our affair, but how can it not be? A man's ill treatment of his wife should be *everyone's* affair."

"You know the truth of it, then," Mrs. Bonner said quietly.

"Of course we know."

Mrs. Bonner turned away. "I am so ashamed."

"And why should you be? It is your husband who bears the shame."

Tommy cried out, and Mrs. Bonner rocked him back and forth in her arms. "I had hoped for just such a son. Oh, I was foolish. But when I read Owen's letters, I dreamed of a family. I thought I would be as happy as Celia Potts when her husband was alive. I brought my mother's silver teapot with me and her best china cups. I have the pot yet, but Owen broke the cups. When I said I would buy new ones once we reached Denver, he asked where I would get the money. 'Why, I have given you my money for safe-keeping,' I told him. He only laughed and said I would never see a penny of it."

"Once we reach Denver, you must leave him," Ma told her again.

"But how can I? He is my husband. Besides, I have just told you, he will not give me back a cent of my money. And without it, what could I do? I can't teach or do laundry, and I don't have the money to open a boarding house. I am even worse prepared to earn my living than Celia. At least she can paint china."

Mrs. Bonner put her cheek against Tommy's before she held him out to Ma.

"We will think of something," Ma said.

She seemed about to say more, when I cried, "Look, mountains! I can see the mountains."

Ma and Mrs. Bonner turned and stared at the western horizon. "Are those really the mountains?" Ma asked. She sounded disappointed, and I was, too, a little. They weren't very impressive, just a line of dark blue. I had seen pictures of mountains in books and thought they were huge snow-covered rocky hills that reached high into the sky.

Pa came up to us then. "Do you see them, the mountains?" he asked us. He sounded very excited. When I said they didn't look like much, he told me, "Just you wait, Emmy Blue. When we get closer, you'll see how big they really are."

"As big as a barn?"

"Bigger than that."

"As big as the bluffs on the Mississippi?"

"Even bigger."

I was doubtful, but Pa never lied, and I would see for myself when we got close to them.

Mrs. Bonner had left us to go back to her wagon, and Ma

said, "I believe her husband will do her great harm one day."

"Crossing the prairie isn't easy for a man," Pa said. "Maybe he'll be all right once he reaches Denver." Then he glanced at Ma. "I know it isn't easy for a woman either. I guess I should have said it isn't easy for anybody."

The oxen had never been so pokey. I prodded them with a stick, but it was almost as if they knew our journey was nearly over and they were slowing down to make it longer. The men with mule-drawn wagons had pulled out of line and moved ahead of us. We passed farms now and way stations where we could buy meals or sleep in beds, but Pa said the food wasn't as good as what we cook over our campfire and the beds most likely had bugs. He didn't want to waste money, either.

At last, Pa pointed to a few log cabins scattered on the prairie. "There it is. Denver."

Ma squinted at the dreary sight. "I thought it would look like Quincy," she said. I could hear the disappointment in her voice.

"Oh, Meggie, don't be discouraged. That's not the main part of the city. It's much finer. Just wait until we get there. You'll see," Pa said.

Buttermilk John told us he would lead us to the Elephant

Corral, which was in the heart of Denver. Then we would be on our own.

"Do they keep elephants there?" I asked. I'd never seen an elephant.

"The Elephant Corral is a stable," Pa explained with a laugh. "It's called that because it's so big."

Soon, Buttermilk John led us through streets that were crowded with prospectors, who were carrying big, round gold pans and picks and shovels. We saw freighters, men who loaded all sorts of things for transports, carrying long whips. There were mountain men like Buttermilk John, wearing suits of deer hide decorated with beads, and bearded men with guns, their chests crisscrossed with leather belts that held bullets. We also saw men in huge aprons standing in front of shops, urging people to come inside and eat. Loud music and laughter came from storefronts. The whole city was crowded and noisy, and after the quiet of the plains, Ma put her hands over her ears to block out the sound. But I liked the excitement. Everywhere I looked, I saw something new.

"Oh, Ma, look," I said as we passed a street of frame-and-log buildings. A wire was stretched across the street, and a woman was balanced on it. She took a step forward, and I cried out, "She'll fall."

Ma stopped and stared, her mouth open. "What is she doing?"

"She's a tightrope walker," Pa said. "She can walk all the way across that wire. She does it every day at noon, or so I've been told."

"Look at the short skirts," I said.

"Why, it's scandalous," Ma told us.

"It's Denver," Pa said, laughing.

When we reached the Elephant Corral, Pa said we'd leave the oxen there for the night and find a place to stay. Golden was ten miles away, so we'd go on in the morning. "I expect you'd like a real bath," he told Ma. "There's enough dirt on all of us to grow wheat!"

"Why, I think I would trade your son for a bath," she replied, and when I looked startled, she added, "That was only a joke, Emmy Blue."

Some of the wagons were continuing on, and we called, "Good luck!" and "Godspeed!" to them.

Mrs. Bonner hurried over to us. "I have some good news," she told us. "We are going to Golden, too. Owen says he will meet some associates there. I believe he wants to go into the mountains later on, but at least I shall have a little more time to spend with my dear friends."

Ma smiled at her. "I hope you can persuade him to stay in Golden."

"That would be my fondest wish," Mrs. Bonner said.

As we talked with Mrs. Bonner, Celia approached, holding Ulysses, with Bert and Honor beside her.

"We are all going to Golden," Aunt Catherine told her. "Would you come there, too, or will you stay in Denver?"

"We would try to find some work for you," Ma added. "Perhaps in a boardinghouse. Thomas says miners will pay a gold nugget to have a shirt washed and ironed by a woman. You could set up a laundry."

Celia shook her head. "How can I, with the care of three children? There is nothing I can do to support us. Besides, I have already made a decision." She smiled a big, genuine, happy smile. The first happy smile we'd seen from her since her husband died. "I am to marry Charlie Pitkin," she told us. "The children and I will go with him and his brother to farm north of here."

"Why?" I burst out without thinking.

Ma touched my arm so that I wouldn't say more. "I thought as much," she told Celia. "He is a good man. You are a fortunate woman."

"I am that," Celia said. "Charlie and Paul have gone to find a clergyman. Charlie and I will be married before the day is out. He will make a good father, and he is gentle. I should like you to stand up with me, Meggie. You have been so good to me that I should like you to be my attendant at the marriage ceremony."

"Of course," Ma said.

Mrs. Bonner hurried to her wagon and returned a few minutes later to present Celia with an embroidered handkerchief.

"You must carry this at your wedding. It is not so much, but it is clean."

"Oh, was there ever a thing so beautiful!" Celia cried.

I had not noticed Ma go to our wagon. Now she climbed down from it, and standing beside Celia, she handed her a folded quilt. "This is for the bride, too," she said, peeling back a corner of the coverlet so that Celia could see the design.

"It's your Dove quilt," I exclaimed.

"And perfect for a bride."

As Celia was admiring the quilt, the Pitkin brothers returned with a man in a long black coat. They introduced him as a reverend, and said that he would perform the ceremony that afternoon at his church.

"But why not right here, in front of our friends?" Celia sounded like her old bustling self.

"Here?" Charlie Pitkin asked.

"Of course," said Celia. "What better way to start a new life than with a ceremony in a place called the Elephant Corral? It will be something to remember when we are old and gray."

"Well, if that's your desire, I suppose we could," Charlie Pitkin said, taking her hand and squeezing it.

So, standing in the mud of the big corral, with oxen moaning and teamsters shouting in the background, Celia married Mr. Charlie Pitkin. Then she and her children climbed into Celia's wagon, and Mr. Pitkin flicked his whip against the oxen to get them moving. Paul Pitkin followed them in his wagon.

"Why, Ma?" I asked, as we watched them go. "Why would she marry him? He's not at all like Mr. Potts."

"She has three children," Ma answered. "And he's a good man. Besides, it's like the scraps of a quilt, Emmy Blue. Sometimes a woman just has to make do."

Chapter Nineteen

THE END OF THE QUILT WALK

$\mathcal{P}$a had been right. I'd never seen anything so big as the mountains west of Golden. They made the bluffs on the Mississippi River look like sand hills. "Those are only the foothills. The real mountains are behind them," Pa told me.

"Are there rivers, too?" I asked.

"Not rivers like the Mississippi or the Missouri, but streams. They rush at you like a steam engine, and they're cold! You wouldn't want to wade in one, even on the hottest summer day," he replied.

Ma had been quiet, and Pa asked, "What do you think of the mountains now, Meggie?"

"I'm not as interested in the mountains and rivers as Emmy Blue. I want to see our home," Ma replied.

We reached the top of a rise, and Pa held up his hand. "Whoa!" he shouted to the oxen. Uncle Will came up beside us and halted his wagon, too. "There it is," Pa yelled. "There's Golden!"

Pa hurried the oxen now, tapping the lead animal on the rump and yelling, "Get along there."

Ma was walking beside the wagon. She took a few steps beyond the oxen and called to Aunt Catherine, "My goodness, Cath. Look at that." I couldn't tell what emotion she was feeling. Aunt Catherine put her hands to her mouth and said she'd never seen a setting so grand.

Ma, Aunt Catherine, and I rushed ahead of the wagons for a closer look at the log cabins, sod huts, and rough shacks that made up the town. Golden's streets were as crowded as Denver's, with freighters loading goods onto wagons. Pa said they were going to the gold camps. Men yelled and laughed, and I heard the sound of a piano.

We'd seen a few two-story brick houses when we went through Denver, but there was nothing like them in Golden. The houses here were rough and unpainted and not at all like the homes we had left behind in Quincy. There wasn't a single house that was as fine as our farmhouse. I glanced at Ma, worried that she was disappointed at the plainness.

We walked into the town, past doors that were open. People called out to each other in a friendly way. Women worked vegetable patches, and I saw flowers everywhere.

Children ran past, barefoot, kicking up the dust in the street. Two boys knelt in the dirt playing marbles, and a girl who was pushing a hoop smiled at me and shouted, "Hi." When she saw Barebones, she held out her hand. "Come here, doggie. Is he yours?"

"His name's Barebones," I said.

"Ain't he swell!" she said, before pushing her hoop ahead of us down the street. I thought Golden was swell, too.

"Well, Meggie?" Pa asked, as he caught up with us.

I looked up at Ma, trying to make out what she was thinking. But Ma's sunbonnet hid her face. Pa was looking at her, too.

"I like it," I said, but Ma didn't respond.

At the end of the street, Pa turned off and stopped the oxen in front of a small house. It was made of logs, but they weren't round. "We squared them off with an ax," Pa explained. The house had a door that was painted red and a window with four panes of glass. There were glass panes in the second story, too. Each window had an iron bar across it to keep intruders from coming in.

"This is our house," Pa said. "It won't be clean inside, because nobody's lived here since I left. I hired a man to keep a watch on it so that nobody would get in and claim it. Folks do that sometimes because buildings are so scarce. But it looks like it's still ours." He took a large iron key from a pocket in the wagon sheet and inserted it into a lock on the door. The key scraped, and Pa and Uncle Will had to jolt the door, but it finally opened.

Ma peered inside, taking in the rough wooden table and chairs and the two beds built into the corners. A cook stove stood at one end. Everything was covered with dust. The floor was dirt.

"Look at the view from the front door," Pa said proudly. "The mountains are on your doorstep."

Ma was quiet. I could tell she was thinking. She walked out back, where Pa showed her the space for her garden, a sunny spot where she could plant the seeds she'd brought along in our medicine chest. She came around to the front again and put her head inside, looking up at the second story.

"There's a ladder inside to reach the loft. That's where Will and Catherine will sleep," Pa explained.

Ma said nothing. She had turned her head to look at the dirt roof. I thought that Ma would never want to live in a house that was dirt top and bottom. But then she began to laugh, the way she had that time Abigail and I had tied Miss Browning's shoelaces together under the table.

Pa looked at her with concern on his face, while I wondered if Ma was so upset at the house that she'd gone crazy.

But at last, Ma caught her breath. "Look at that, Emmy Blue," she said, and pointed to the roof of the house. Dandelions and bluebells and red blossoms that Pa called Indian paintbrush were growing on the dirt roof, along with other flowers whose names I didn't know. There were so many that the top of the house was a blaze of color. "We have flowers blooming on our roof. Did you ever see such a funny sight? Wait until I write Grandma Mouse about it. She will be charmed." She chuckled a little, and then shook her head. "I believe I could live in a house that has a roof of flowers, a roof that makes me laugh. Come inside, Emmy Blue."

"I am beholden to you, Meggie, for coming all this way and being such a dutiful wife," Pa said. He grinned at me, then whispered, "I guess your ma's going to stay."

"She has a stout heart," I told him.

Pa nodded. "I knew it all along."

And then Ma said to me, "This is the end of your quilt walk, Emmy Blue. We are home."

Chapter Twenty

RESCUING MRS. BONNER

"*I* believe I will like this place, this Golden," Ma told Aunt Catherine and me as we cleaned the cabin.

"There isn't much to housekeeping in a home this size," Aunt Catherine replied with a smile, her hands smudged with the blacking she was rubbing onto the cook stove. "We are going to have to sit on the bed while we cook."

That day, we brushed the cobwebs off the ceiling, washed the walls and the furniture, and swept the floor, though Aunt Catherine pointed out there wasn't much use to sweeping since the floor was dirt.

We met one of our neighbors on our first day in Golden, too. We were making up the beds when a woman from across the road came over with a loaf of bread still warm from the oven. "Wheat bread was the thing I longed for most during my months on the trail," she said. "You just can't bake it properly over a campfire. The first day I was here, I knocked on the door of a stranger and asked if I could use her oven for my bread. She understood."

Ma had just unfolded her Feathered Star quilt to spread on her bed, and the woman peered at it. "God bless me, I can see you piece. And such lovely work." She lifted a corner of the quilt and studied the stitches. "I brought four quilt tops with me, thinking I'd finish them here, but there's not a place where I can find batting or muslin for the backing."

Ma frowned at that. "No place to buy yard goods? I've never heard such a thing. Isn't there a general store?"

"Yes, but all it stocks is shoddy, that cheap fabric that falls apart with one washing, and that at high prices."

"I promised my daughter that as soon as we were settled, I would buy her a piece of material to back the little quilt she made on the trail," Ma said. "And I would dearly love to make myself a dress or two. You see, there wasn't room in the wagon for my clothes, so I had to wear them all for much of our trip. Now, instead of one worn-out dress, I have three. Women here will think I'm shoddy, too."

Our neighbor only laughed. "Why, if you had new dresses, we'd think you were putting on airs. You'll find things are different here. We don't judge. We take folks as they are." She started back to her cabin, then called over her shoulder.

"I've been baking pies. I'll bring you one for your supper if you don't mind. It's no botheration."

"Dried apple pie?" I asked.

"Oh, heavens no. Pie plant."

I didn't understand, and Ma whispered, "Rhubarb."

The woman smiled. "It was the first thing I planted when I came here two years ago. I couldn't look another dried apple pie in the face."

After the woman left, Ma said, "Did you hear that, Cath? She said there's not a place in Golden to buy yard goods. I guess we will have to tear up our dresses for scraps for our quilts."

"But first, we must find dresses to replace them," Aunt Catherine said.

We were busy that first week, arranging the cabin, planting a late June garden, and cooking the things we had all missed on the trail. It wasn't until several days after we arrived that we had time to visit the stores.

"That's my only disappointment with Golden," Ma said after we left the general store. "There are plenty of gold pans and men's overalls and work boots, but not a thing for a woman to stitch." The store had three bolts of fabric, which Ma had asked the clerk to take down. She'd fingered each one, then shook her head. "They wouldn't survive a washing," she said.

"Suit yourself," the shopkeeper had told her. "You'll find no better."

As we walked along the streets, Ma glanced this way and that. At first, I thought she was looking for a dry goods store. But then she paused and stared at a woman climbing down from a wagon. Ma took a step toward her, then stopped and told Aunt Catherine, "It's not her."

"Who?" I asked.

"Mrs. Bonner. I thought she would have arrived in Golden by now. Perhaps their plans have changed."

"I suppose we shall never learn," Aunt Catherine said.

But as it turned out, we did learn.

Pa and Uncle Will had already started building the business block. While Ma, Aunt Catherine, and I took care of the house, Pa and Uncle Will used our oxen to grade the building site that Pa had purchased more than a year before. They needed help, so they went to The Prospector, a saloon and gambling hall, where someone had told them the bartender kept a list of men looking for work.

The first person they saw when they went inside, Pa later told us, was Mr. Bonner. He was sitting at a table, drunk as a pigeon, playing cards. Pa said he tried to ignore him, but Mr. Bonner spotted him, threw his cards on the table and greeted Pa like he was an old friend. "Hatchett, you're just the man I want to see."

Pa turned away and went to the bar to ask for the list of workmen, but Mr. Bonner followed him, Pa said.

"I could use the loan of a twenty-dollar gold piece. I'm a good poker player, but I have had a string of bad luck. That or someone over there is cheating."

"Sorry. I haven't got twenty dollars to spare," Pa told him.

"Ten then."

Pa shook his head.

Mr. Bonner sneered at him. "I guess that means I'll have to put my wife to work," he said, looking around him. "There's always work for women in these places."

Pa told us how angry he got at what Mr. Bonner said, "You would force your wife to work in a saloon? She is a lady."

Pa turned around, walked out of the saloon, his hands balled into fists. "I was afraid I would hit him," Pa told us.

"Poor Lucy," Ma said. "I wish we could help. He'll wear her out if she lives long enough."

"It's not our business," Pa said.

The next morning, Pa and Uncle Will went to work early, as usual, but Pa didn't come home for dinner. Uncle Will explained that Pa had gone on an errand. Late in the day, Pa came to the cabin and said to Ma, Aunt Catherine, and me, "Come with me, all three of you."

"Whatever for?" Ma asked.

"You'll see." Pa led us to the edge of town where several covered wagons were parked. "Wait here," he said, as he climbed onto the wheel of one and called, "It's Thomas Hatchett."

"Go away. Please," Mrs. Bonner said in a voice so low that we could barely hear her.

"I've brought my wife and my sister-in-law, and Emmy Blue, too."

"No. I can't see them."

Ma gestured for Pa to get down, then she stepped onto the wagon spoke and said, "Lucy, it's Meggie."

"No."

That didn't stop Ma. She climbed into the wagon and exclaimed, "Why, the monster! What has he done to your arm?"

"I fell."

"No, he pushed you, or worse. And what about the fresh bruises? Oh. Lucy, come with us. Surely anything is better than this."

"Where could I go? I'd be disgraced," Mrs. Bonner said.

"You could go with us. We will take you in. And, disgraced? This is Golden. People in Colorado Territory are not so taken with convention as they were back home. I've learned that already. They would know your husband's treatment of you is not your fault."

Ma drew Mrs. Bonner to the edge of the wagon. As Mrs.

Bonner came into the sunlight, she bumped her arm against her side and winced.

"Mrs. Bonner, you can sleep in Emmy Blue's bed with her. You are coming home with us."

"I would be such a burden," Mrs. Bonner said, but she let Ma lead her from the wagon.

"Your ill treatment by your husband would be a greater burden on us," Pa replied. "Meggie is right. We should have insisted you leave Mr. Bonner the moment you reached Denver."

Ma helped Mrs. Bonner to the ground, then Pa climbed back into her wagon and removed the sacks and boxes that contained her things, and we all carried them down the street to our cabin. As we were walking along, Pa told us, "I searched all day for her."

"You did the right thing," Ma said. "Lucy is in misery so deep she can hardly talk. But what if Mr. Bonner comes after her?"

"I did some checking around. It seems Bonner is a known card cheat and troublemaker, and he is not welcome in Golden. The sheriff promised to talk to him as soon as Mrs. Bonner was safely in our hands. He'll tell Bonner to leave, or else he'll get thrown into jail. He'll let him know that if any harm comes to Mrs. Bonner, the men of Golden will see to him."

"You've said all along that we should not interfere. What

changed your mind, Thomas?" Ma asked.

Pa smiled at her. "My wife was willing to give up her family and old friends to start a new life with me, a change she didn't want to make. I got to thinking it was only right I change, too, and that meant interfering in something that isn't my business. Your friend's life is worth a little change of mind."

If I had to think of something good to say about Mr. Bonner, it was that he did not make his wife wear all of her dresses at one time as she crossed the prairie. She brought trunks of clothes with her in the wagon. The first thing she did after she moved into our cabin was to give dresses to Ma and Aunt Catherine, much to their delight.

"We are so grateful to you. Our old clothes are in tatters now, all of them," Ma said. "We will save the good parts for scraps, and the rest will do for rags."

With the new dresses ready to be worn, Ma ripped up the old ones. She clipped the places that were not worn and cut them into diamonds for a star quilt. She saved one large square of fabric and said it would do for the backing of my Indian Rescue quilt. I had already stitched the squares together, so one afternoon, she cut a piece from one of my old dresses to fit Waxy's quilt top. Ma, Mrs. Bonner, Aunt

Catherine, and I sat in the yard, quilting the top to the back.

"There's nothing to use for a batting between the two layers, except rags, and Waxy's quilt is too good for that. So we'll skip the batting. This will be a summer quilt," Ma said. She shook her head. "I never knew a town that didn't sell batting."

There was no quilt frame either, so the four of us passed around the little quilt, each taking a few stitches.

"It's too bad there's not a special store where you can buy yard goods and batting and needles and such," I said. The remark surprised me, and I wondered if I was beginning to like sewing.

"Yes, a pity," Ma replied, then stopped her stitching. She turned to Mrs. Bonner. "That is exactly the solution to your dilemma, Lucy. You can open a sewing store that sells just what Emmy Blue mentioned. There isn't a woman in Golden who wouldn't be thrilled to have a place to buy yard goods. Now they have to write home for what they want, and it takes months before the goods arrive. You could sell calico and muslin, Lucy, maybe even silk and velvet later on if there is a demand for it. You could stock all the findings, too—buttons and snaps and twill tape, thimbles and thread, even trimmings. If there's room, you could put up a quilt frame in the store so that women could set-in their quilts to be stitched."

"And you would not only sell supplies to women but help them with their stitching. You are so clever with your needle," Aunt Catherine said. "Before long, you could have them doing embroidery and tatting, too—all with supplies they've purchased from you, of course."

"But I've never run a shop before," Mrs. Bonner said.

"You'd never gone west before, either, but you got here. Catherine and I would help you. Emmy Blue, too." Ma looked at my stitches on Waxy's quilt. "Perhaps not so much with sewing, but Emmy Blue could stock shelves and help with customers."

"I have a little money that I got from selling some of the things in the wagon," Mrs. Bonner said slowly.

"Then it's all set," Ma told her.

"But where would I set up shop? I haven't seen a vacant store in all of Golden."

Ma's eyes twinkled. "You leave that to me."

That night, we left Tommy with Aunt Catherine, and Ma and Pa and I went for a walk along Clear Creek. We didn't have a well yet, so we had to haul the water we used. Each of us carried a pail. When we reached the creek, Ma sat down on a rock and looked up at the sky. "There are thousands of stars, maybe more than that, but the mountains get in the way," she said.

"Do you like the mountains now?" Pa asked dipping a

bucket into the cold creek.

"They are comforting, especially at night. They are like having warm arms around me." Ma sighed, then was silent for a moment, before she said, "I believe we have found an occupation for Lucy." She talked slowly, as if she were choosing her words carefully. "She will open a shop that will sell yard goods and trims and findings. Women who have worn out their clothes traveling a thousand miles across the prairie will be anxious to make new ones. And they will want to go to quilting, too. There's nothing that will make a cabin a home faster than bright quilts on the beds."

Pa shrugged. "I don't know much about such things."

"We have checked around, the three of us"—she glanced at me—"the four of us, that is. There isn't a woman who wouldn't patronize such a shop. Of course, it will take a few months for the goods to arrive, so Lucy will have time to get everything ready."

Pa stared at Clear Creek, which sent up white foam as it rushed over the rocks. In the moonlight, the foam looked like ice. He didn't seem to be paying much attention as he dipped another pail into the water.

"There is just one problem," Ma said.

Pa stopped, the pail only half filled.

"We need to find a place for Lucy's store. We have looked all over Golden, and there isn't a spot available. With the way Golden is booming, any store space is taken up the moment it is finished. I don't know where in the world Lucy could open her shop."

Pa turned to look at Ma then, his head cocked, waiting.

Ma smiled at him. "She wouldn't need much space, Thomas, and you have room for several stores in that building."

"But the space has all been promised. It will be much more profitable if we rent to a hardware store or a restaurant or a saloon."

"A saloon!" Ma said. "Surely, you aren't serious, Thomas."

"I am. A saloon pays better than a bank. In fact, the space is already let. There's nothing wrong with a well-run saloon. Where else would you expect men to go after a day's work underground?" He added, "I doubt Lucy Bonner would want to be next door to such an establishment."

"No." Ma thought a moment. "But she could be upstairs. You could build a stairway on the side of the building. I don't imagine you could rent that space to a saloon or any other business."

"A lawyer or a doctor, maybe."

"Lucy would pay every bit as much in rent, and her clients wouldn't spit tobacco juice on the floor," Ma said.

"Would women climb the stairs?"

"Women would climb a mountain to buy fabric for their quilts!"

"I don't know, Meggie. I don't like the idea of a woman renting from me."

Ma turned to face Pa, her hands on her hips, "You listen to me, Thomas. A woman's money is every bit as good as a man's. When we arrived in Golden, you said you were beholden to me for giving up everything I cared about and for following you west. You said I was a dutiful wife. Now it is your turn to be a dutiful husband. I want you to rent that space to Lucy."

Pa took a step backward, and still tending to a bucket, he put up his hands in surrender, water sloshing down his arms. Then he turned to me, the corners of his mouth lifted just a little. "Your ma does indeed have a stout heart."

Chapter Twenty-One

THE QUILT THAT
WALKED TO GOLDEN

$\mathcal{M}$a and Aunt Catherine soaked in the afternoon sunlight that came through the windows in Mrs. Bonner's shop, Golden Sewing Supplies. It was in an upstairs room of what Pa had named the Hatchett Block. The frame was small, and every so often, the women stood to roll up a completed section and expose a new portion of the quilt. Ma looked down at Tommy, who was sleeping in a basket beside her, then stretched and sat down again beside Aunt Catherine.

Mrs. Bonner picked up her needle and took several tiny stitches, but before she could pull the thread through the fabric sandwich of quilt top, batting, and backing, she stood up to greet a customer. It had been like that all afternoon. Mrs. Bonner would take a few stitches, then someone would climb the stairs to the store and ask for a spool of thread or a yard of calico.

"Emmy Blue, do you want to sit down and stitch for a few minutes?" Ma asked.

I had been putting away thimbles and buttons and spools of thread. This was Mrs. Bonner's second shipment of merchandise. The first had all but sold out in a month. She paid me a dollar a week to help in the store after school and on Saturdays. "I have to finish this," I said, and Ma and Aunt Catherine smiled. They knew I was better at stocking shelves than I was at sewing. I smiled back at them, as I placed the egg-rock on a paper pattern to keep it from blowing away. The egg-rock was the one that Joey had given me when he left our wagon train, and I had, in turn, given it to Mrs. Bonner the day the store opened. It was for good luck, I'd explained.

Ma ran her hand over the quilt she was working on. It was a giant star, made from pieces of the dresses we'd worn on the overland trail. "Remember this one, Cath?" She tapped her finger on a white sprig on a black background. "That was going to be my best dress when I reached Golden."

"And this red was from Emmy Blue's middle dress."

"Back in Quincy, you made a dress for Waxy from those yard goods, too," I said. "She still has hers. Waxy wasn't as hard on her clothes as I was."

"Nobody is," Ma said with a smile.

Aunt Catherine held up a green diamond shape. "That's

the dress that was scorched in the campfire the first week of our trip. I learned to be careful after that," she recalled.

Mrs. Bonner finished helping her customer, who admired the quilt before she left. She also told Ma she'd be back later in the week to give her a hand with the stitching.

"You'd better hurry up and finish before she comes back," Mrs. Bonner said after the woman was gone. "She takes toenail stitches." When Ma didn't understand, Mrs. Bonner explained. "Stitches big enough to catch your big toe. You'd have to take them out."

We all laughed. I glanced around the shop. It was small, and it still smelled of newly sawed wood, but it was cheerful, with the bright bolts of fabric stacked on shelves, the glass case of multicolor trims, and Ma's quilt on the wall. The day Mrs. Bonner opened for business, Ma had brought her Friendship Quilt to hang in the shop. "Whenever I sit here to quilt," she had said, "I can look up at it and remember my friends. And one or two of your customers might get the idea they would want one. Where do you suppose they would buy the fabrics for it?" She'd grinned.

Now Ma looked at Mrs. Bonner, who was so happy she almost glowed. She hadn't seen Mr. Bonner since the day she came to live with us. "Never should I have married such a man, but he's gone out of my remembrance now," she'd told us.

"I expect we can finish this quilt today," Ma told Mrs.

Bonner. She tapped her foot to the piano music that came through the floor. "Who would have thought I'd be doing my quilting over a saloon. But I like the music. It's snappy."

Pa had rented to a saloon. There was a bank in the space next to it, and two doctors and a lawyer rented space upstairs from it, next to the sewing shop. It was a grand building, two stories high, made of brick and wood, with plate glass windows in front. Ma had written to Grandma Mouse that the Hatchett Block was a great success.

Tommy woke up and cried a little. Ma started to put aside her needle, but I said I'd take care of him. I picked him up and said, "Look at that big quilt, Tommy." But he only sniffled, no more interested in quilting than I'd been back in Quincy. I jiggled the baby and showed him to Barebones, who was stretched out nearby. In a moment, I laid Tommy in his basket, where he fell asleep.

I went back to my work, listening to Ma, Aunt Catherine, and Mrs. Bonner. Although I still wasn't crazy about stitching, I liked the talk that went on around the quilt frame—the friendliness. I decided that was the best part of quilting.

At last, the three women stood up and loosened the quilt. Ma took it out of the frame and held it up. "Done!" she said. The women clapped, and Barebones thumped his tail.

The quilt was a single large star made up of hundreds of diamond shapes cut from the dresses we'd worn on our trip from Quincy to Golden. It was a happy quilt, and I thought it would always remind me of my quilt walk across the plains. Looking back on it, I decided that quilting as I walked along beside the wagons hadn't been such a bad thing. In fact, I'd almost enjoyed it.

"What is that pattern?" Mrs. Bonner asked.

"I believe it's called Lone Star," Aunt Catherine told her.

"What an ordinary name. We can do better than that," Mrs. Bonner said.

"We could call it Starry Night on the Prairie," Ma said. "I loved lying on the ground and looking up at the stars. I believe that's why I made another star quilt."

"Or Prairie Star," Aunt Catherine suggested.

Ma nodded. "Something like that." She ran her hand over the star. "Who would believe the pieces of this quilt came from the dresses we wore one on top of the other as we walked beside the wagons on our way to Golden?"

"That's it, Ma," I said. I shoved a bolt of cloth into place.

"That's what, Emmy Blue?"

"The name of the quilt."

"I don't understand," Ma said. "What name?"

I went over to the quilt then and touched a diamond that had come from the fabric of the first dress I'd put on that last morning in Quincy, a blue calico. "This quilt shouldn't have a star name at all," I said. "We are going to call it The Quilt That Walked to Golden."

A NOTE FROM THE AUTHOR

There really was a quilt that walked. The girl who may have made it was Alice Burgess. In 1864, Alice's father, Thomas Burgess, and his brother, Jacob, set out from Ohio for Golden, Colorado. The two men planned to build a business block, which would provide space for stores and offices. The two Burgess wagons were filled with building supplies, and the brothers told their wives—both of them named Mary—there was no room for clothing. The women would be allowed to take only what they could wear. So the two wives put on all their dresses, one on top of another, and they all set out for Colorado.

Because riding in a wagon was boring and the seat was hard, the women walked most of the way. Alice probably walked, too. Family legend says that after the clothes wore out, Mary Jane, Thomas's wife, cut them into diamond shapes and made a quilt of them. The quilt was known as The Quilt that Walked to Golden. It is now in the collection of the Rocky Mountain Quilt Museum in Golden, Colorado.

Like many quilt stories, this one seems to be as much legend as fact. Some of the fabrics in the quilt were not manufactured until long after 1864. And while Mary Jane probably cut out many of its pieces, the quilt may have been put together after her death, by her daughter or granddaughter.

Nobody really knows for sure. The combination of truth and family stories is what makes quilt history fun.

I wrote about Mary Jane Burgess and her quilt in my 2004 history of Colorado quilting, *The Quilt That Walked to Golden*. Jacob and his wife, Mary, left Golden before 1870. Thomas and Mary Jane stayed on for many years with their daughter, Alice, as well as two sons. Thomas operated the Burgess Block as a saloon, store, and public hall. Later it became a hotel and restaurant. The building at 1015 Ford Street still stands. It has been turned into apartments.

When I wrote *The Quilt That Walked to Golden*, I was intrigued by the girl, Alice. What would the trip have been like for her? Did she have adventures on the way? Did she help her mother cut up dresses for the Star Quilt? And did she eventually become a quilter herself? Information about Alice and her family is sketchy. I wanted to know more about her. So when Amy Lennex, senior editor at Sleeping Bear Press, approached me about writing a children's book, I jumped at the chance to create a girl who walks across the prairie with her family to Colorado.

Although *The Quilt Walk* is based on a real incident in Colorado history, the book is mostly a work of fiction. That's why I changed the names. I thought it wasn't fair to make up stories about real people. So Alice became Emmy Blue, and her parents became Meggie and Thomas Hatchett. Emmy Blue's adventures came from my imagination.

ACKNOWLEDGMENTS

While I've published eleven novels, I'd never written a children's book and couldn't have done it without the direction and support of Amy Lennex. She worked with me page by page to make Emmy Blue and her story come alive. I'm also grateful to Audrey Macks Mitnick, senior publicist at Sleeping Bear, and to my wonderful agents, Danielle Egan-Miller and Joanna MacKenzie of Browne & Miller Literary Associates, who encouraged me to take on this project. Emmy Blue couldn't have better friends than the four of you.

And I couldn't have better friends than Bob, Dana, Kendal, Lloyd, and Forrest. They are the reason I write about the love and support of families. Forrest, *The Quilt Walk* is for you and your friends.

ABOUT THE AUTHOR

Sandra Dallas is the author of eleven novels and ten nonfiction books for adults. With *The Quilt Walk*, she brings her much-admired storytelling talent to young readers for the first time.

Sandra graduated with a degree in journalism from the University of Denver, and began her writing career as a reporter with *Business Week*. A staff member for twenty-five years, and the magazine's first female bureau chief, she covered the Rocky Mountain region. Many of her experiences have been incorporated into her novels.

Sandra is the recipient of the Women Writing the West® Willa Literary Award, the National Cowboy Hall of Fame Wrangler Award, and is a two-time winner of the Western Writers of America Spur Award. She has been awarded a Romantic Times Reviewers' Choice Award for Historical Fiction. In addition, she has been a finalist for the Colorado Book Award, the Mountains & Plains Independent Booksellers Association Award, and the Romantic Times Reviewers' Choice Award.

Sandra lives in Colorado with her husband.